# *Earthy Existentialism*

# by Patricia Herron

In daily experience, and in this book, stories, lyric moments, and resonant ideas call to us, and if we attend to them, life becomes a buoyant struggle. *Earthy Existentialism* will enrich you, haunt you, engage your mind and heart—like memories of resonant episodes you haven't lived, until now.

—**Kim Stafford**, author of *Having Everything Right: Essays of Place*
Director, Northwest Writing Institute, Lewis & Clark College

*Earthy Existentialism*, a new multi-genre collection by Patricia Herron, is packed with what she calls her "truth-seeking intellectual explorations." Gleaned from a lifetime of living, writing, philosophizing, and teaching, Herron assures readers that she always tries to "bridge theory, experience, and story." Elaborating on that approach, she explains that "abstract categories must find expression and grounding in narrative chronicles." So, Herron, a philosophy professor, former ranch wife and single mother of four, invites the reader to follow her eight narratives populated with an amazing cast of largely rural characters: a mentally retarded girl, cock fighters, innocent boys, cowboys, loggers, horsemen, goat herds, bull elk, black horses, dying men, old women, a remote university, philosophy students, and godly professors. Once her stories, rich with philosophical and autobiographical allusions, are told, Herron uses her four essays to interpret the events and characters in those narratives and to comment on their significance in multiple philosophical traditions—Plato to Heidegger. To conclude, she shares a sheaf of eight short meditative poems written while a single mother living in a remote cabin in Indian Valley outside Elgin, Oregon. With these three genres, Herron seeks to share her years of thinking and living and to enlighten any reader with her love of words, images, and most of all—ideas.

--**George Venn,** author of *Beaver's Fire*, and
*Marking the Magic Circle*
Professor of English (retired), Eastern Oregon University

Some people long to rise above the messiness of life. Others are content with wallowing in it. Patricia Herron is one of the rare souls who understand, as she says in this book, "One cannot safely go high unless one also visits the depths." She pursues philosophy as the ancient Greeks intended: as a way of life. In *Earthy Existentialism* Herron blends gritty tales of growing up in eastern Oregon with refined meditations on Heidegger, consciousness, and spirituality. This is a unique book, because Patricia Herron is a unique seeker of truth: a woman who has an equally strong attraction to what is, and what ought to be; to the here-and-now, and to the eternal.

**--Brian Hines,** Author, *Return to the One*,
and *God's Whisper, Creation's Thunder*

In *Earthy Existentialism*, Patricia Herron writes abstract philosophy, but she also feels we need to ground abstract ideas in narratives of actual lived experience. For this, she also writes fiction, exploring her characters' situations and dilemmas in gritty, emotionally honest ways that can also relate back to the terms of philosophy. Her mind traverses from abstract to concrete and back again with ease. Herron is no intellectual dilettante. Her interest in spiritual matters is derived from direct experience, and this experience shapes her approach to both ideas and art.

**--James Lough, Ph.D.,** Professor, Department of Writing
Savannah College of Art and Design

Critical and analytical writing is usually kept separate from creative writing, and genres of the latter are likewise kept separate from each other. This separation makes it seem as if there were no connection between the mental activities that generate analytical essays, short stories, and poems. Occasionally, a book appears in which the different sorts of verbal makings of one mind are gathered together. In Oregon, a distinguished example of this is George Venn's 1987 volume, *Marking the Magic Circle: An Intimate Geography*, included in the list of the state's 100 Best Books 1800-2000. Patricia Herron's *Earthy Existentialism: Stories, Poems, and Essays from the Wisdom of Eastern Oregon* is another such gathering. As its title signals, Herron, like Venn, locates herself firmly in a world centered in Eastern Oregon. As with Venn, this centering, this digging in, is a way of reaching out, and the gathering together of works in both imaginative and analytical modes is a way of showing that ideas are, or can and should be, deeply part of lived experience.

--**Eleanor Berry,** Author of *Green November* & *No Constant Hues*
Past President, Oregon Poetry Association
Past President, National Federation of State Poetry Societies


Patricia Herron is a philosopher whose heart and mind have been in dialog all her adult life, and that conversation is a moving and rich one. ***Earthy Existentialism*** is the engaging record of that conversation. It is shaped by Pat's life in eastern OR, her single-motherhood, her embrace of philosophy in university life and beyond, and all that was in between. It is full of the wisdom that emerges when life's different directions come together.

--**Flo Leibowitz,** School of History,
Philosophy and Religion, Oregon State University

# Earthy Existentialism:
## Stories, Poems, and Essays
## from the Grit &Wisdom
## of Eastern Oregon

by

# Patricia Herron

HER (Hakomi Educational Resources) Press
Mill City, Oregon USA

Grateful acknowledgment is made to the following for permission to reprint previously published material:  Reflection on "Leave Taking" and Heidegger (with Bindamen) by *The Humanistic Psychologist*.

**Herron, Patricia**, 1940-
*Earthy Existentialism*:  *Stories, Poems, and Essays from the Grit*
          *&Wisdom of Eastern Oregon*
Includes: Short Stories, Poems, Philosophical Essays, plus
          Bibliographic References.

For more information contact the publisher, HER (Hakomi Educational Resources) Press, at Post Office Box 23, Mill City, Oregon 97360, or call 1 (503) 871-8641.

# Table of Contents

## *Poems* and Prose

# Essays

# Forward
## by
## Thomas Madden[1]

Although many writers excel in one area of literature—for instance poetry, the short story, or the essay-- very few become skilled practitioners in more than one area. Patricia Herron is one of these rare people. She is a writer, thinker, and artist who transcends conventional genre boundaries with ease, making a very difficult task look easy. In *Earthy Existentialism,* Patricia showcases for us a significant body of work in three major genres of writing: The short story, the philosophical essay, and poetry. This is a major achievement, and even more so when we consider that, for reasons of space, this book can't accommodate a selection of her work in two other genres, one of them outside writing altogether. Patricia's book *Spheres of Awareness,* a collection of essays on the philosopher Ken Wilber she co-edited with James Lough, reveals her as a talented editor and midwife for the work of other writers. And her work as a visual artist, as the creator of many striking and symbolic acrylic paintings, demonstrates, again, how skillfully she can transcend the limitations of genre.

In addition to her fine work in these multiple genres, Patricia also demonstrates another rare talent in *Earthy Existentialism*: She imbues every aspect of her work with a set of unifying themes, a point of focus, a central core around which everything she writes revolves. That central theme, which she approaches and discusses from several different directions, might best be summarized as the constant human drive to move beyond the "Is" toward the "Ought," to edge our common everyday selves into a relationship with, in her terms, "a Larger, Organic, or Ultimate Self." (p. 159). These comments come from one of her essays in this book, "The 'I-I's Have It." Elsewhere in that essay,

---

[1] Retired head of the English Department at Eastern Oregon University where he taught English, writing, and journalism for twenty-five years. Author of two collections of poems: *Graves in Wheat* (Ice River Press, 1998), *and Lessons for Custer* (Wordcraft of Oregon, 2006). It is noted with sadness that Tom Madden died after writing this Forward before the book came to publication.

1

she adds: "I claim that...the messiness of consciousness is necessary in order for the Ultimate Source to be firmly rooted in the world (p. 161). "

Patricia illustrates this "messiness" of everyday life in her short stories, many of which are set in gritty rural locations, and often portray individuals behaving cruelly or thoughtlessly toward other people or animals. Again, and again in these stories we encounter human beings or animals caught up in difficult situations, struggling to get beyond the limitations of their daily lives.

Because they don't always get out of these situations well or cleanly, there is often a tragic dimension: A sense of foreboding, of frustration, of loss. But the reader (if not always the characters) usually gets a glimpse, no matter how dark the circumstances might be, of some better place or situation that might be possible, even if seemingly out of reach for now.

Striving for that place can become a major drive for characters in the stories, for instance in the story "For the Good of Mazie." In this story, the central character is Mazie, a middle-aged woman living in eastern Oregon who, because of an accident in her youth, is brain-damaged and has difficulty functioning in the "normal" world. As the story immerses us in the "messiness" of Mazie's life, we also see that she is a seeker and a striver:

She, like everyone else, is trying to find a "still point" or center to her life. In the process, thinking she might be helping a neighbor who stages cock-fights, she brings a number of tame roosters to a match. These are not fighters, and some of them do not survive. We are left wondering, as Mazie views the bodies of the dead roosters and the huddled survivors, what she has learned from this experience. Part of the story's power is that we, the readers, remain curious about what goodness or insight Mazie has achieved—and how we might apply this story to our own lives.

In another story, "Ranch Infused Philosophy," the main character, Anne, a philosophy teacher in La Grande in northeast Oregon, pays a visit to the family ranch near Elgin, a small town near La Grande.

The story becomes a meditation by Anne on how difficult it is to teach abstract philosophical ideas to students, who are, again, caught up in the "messiness" of their own lives. After visiting with her son, who runs the ranch, and watching him work with horses and do other ranch chores, Anne reflects that he seems perfectly blended with his environment. Anne thinks that her son seems to exist as a child of the Tao, a Taoist hermit. No attachment to beliefs, theories, or fanfare; just riding the waves of the Tao, the energy and force of God, without adhering to dogma of any sort (p. 115).

So, Anne concludes her meditation wondering if she can now build a bridge between the daily lives of her students and the ideas of the philosophers—ideas that, although they may sometimes seem divorced from life, develop and grow from the thoughtful analysis of that same everyday "messy" human experience.

Another story of Patricia's, "Leave Taking," forms a helpful connection between her fiction writing and her philosophical essays, because she has written an essay commenting on this story and linked it to key ideas of the 20th-century philosopher Martin Heidegger. In the story, Maggie, an older woman, is nearing the end of her life and her problematic relationship with her husband of many years, Willy. She spends the last afternoon of her life tending her roses, and then takes to her bed.

As she prepares to die, she reflects not only on how she and Willy have grown apart, but also on her current state of transition and Willy's apparent inability to understand what is really happening to her. Although he gives her a rose from the garden, Willy remains stuck in his everyday routines and habits, wrapped up in himself, while she begins to experience the great change she is about to undergo.

She is now moving from the "messiness" of the everyday world into a new dimension. Patricia tells us that at this point in her life, Maggie experiences what the philosopher Heidegger calls "essential thinking," the ability to perceive the world and time in terms of intensive particularity and individuality—and at the same time to the potential that experience reflects both "everything and nothing."

As she contemplates what she is experiencing, Maggie reflects that all the events of these last hours seem to be coming together: "How very splendid to be summoned down, down, and then up, up and then it was…all rose, all everything, and all nothing (p. 129)."

As Patricia explains, Maggie's words indicate a relationship between death and the essential nature of our thinking, which is simply a kind of thinking that allows particular beings to exist in their particularity: "the rose is . . . death is and Maggie is (p. 129)."

In the essay already referred to, "The I-Is Have It," Patricia approaches this question of particularity from another direction. She acknowledges that the body and mind may be made up of "composite minerals" that can be studied by science, but she adds:

> [t]he great situation of humankind cannot be so easily defined. The problems that are expressed in anguish, in mental suffering, arise out of the experience of the conflict between existence and expectation: "Who are we and what is our destiny? . . . . We must discern the difference between the phenomenal self, the messiness of consciousness . . . and the high-er Self as described by the mystics (p. 163)."

Patricia also reminds us that: We are immersed in perplexities because we come out of the world, like leaves from a tree. We cannot step out of the world, although we attempt to do so when we reach for objective satisfaction. Too often we attempt to explain our situation as the "'What we Are' in the same sense that one would explain a leaf or a rock…. (p. 163)"

A keynote for Patricia in this essay and elsewhere in her writing is that our human consciousness can evolve, grow deeper, more inclusive, more complex. And to make this process work, she insists that we use all our experience, including the most mundane or trivial. As she says, "one cannot safely go high unless one also visits the depths." (p. 167) And she concludes: "My…claim is that the 'Ought' is founded upon the 'Is.'" It is founded on the "Is" because without this grounding in the nat-

4

ural world and the consequent natural laws, the stories of our lives are told with naiveté and narcissism (p. 167).

It is in Patricia's poems that we can find an even more direct route from the everyday "messiness" to the reality of the Ultimate Source that the mystics discuss.

The poems included in *Earthy Existentialism* were written while Patricia lived with her family on a house on Indian Creek near Elgin, and they all reflect her deep interest in the natural world. They also illustrate how intensively she viewed these natural scenes as symbols of deeper realities—windows, as it were, into, the world of the "Ought" she discusses so frequently in her work. One poem, "A Walk," recounts an excursion to a rock on a hill overlooking her house and the surrounding country. She sits down on the rock and then describes what she sees:

> `Below I can see a town, barn, trees and
> The mountains overlooking…
> An autumn breeze is gently blowing,
> And a magpie is calling it's caw outward…
> Leaves are red and yellow,
> The stubborn ones remain green…
> As she sits quietly, she hears:
> Shriek of the hawks.
> And behind me a squeaky
> Chant belonging to
> The insect world.
> A task it seems again to me.
> A job being done, life's own way
> Of completing itself (pp. 189-90).

"A Walk," summarizes Patricia's major themes and forms the capstone of her achievements in this book. By gently fusing the everyday natural world with the symbolic world of the Ought, she shares her sense of the power and energy of that fusion in way that brings us a fresh vision of this daily world of experience we live in, confronting both the "messiness" of it and the beauty behind it, and showing us how they can become one and the same. As we begin to read and to ponder Patricia's fine book, her poem "A Walk" is an excellent place to begin the journey.

# Editor's Preface
by
## Gregory J. Johanson, Ph.D.[2]

I first met Patricia Herron by chance in a Starbucks inside of a Safeway; or if one's theory of consciousness extends far enough, perhaps not so chancy. I was innocently sitting, reading and underlining a book, assisted by my tall coffee (cream, no sugar.) Out of the corner of my eye I become aware of a mature woman stepping my way, who stops, and exclaims. "Oh, you underline your books, just like I do."

Immediately, I assess possible escape routes, and graceful ways out of this unexpected intrusion into my introverted time in my semi-private cave. This unknown being could be one of several possibilities, some happier than others. But something tips the scale toward engaging and exploring more. "So, you're into books, too.?"

"Yes," and all of a sudden we are fast into a discussion that reveals we have many common interests in such things as the philosophy of religion that she has taught in various colleges, as well as many books and subjects, since my own background is in the philosophy and psychology of religion. In particular, we are probably the only two people in a fifty-mile radius who have published works related to the Integral Philosophy of Ken Wilber. Plus, it turns out she was raised on a ranch in a small town in Eastern Oregon named Elgin. I am one of few people in the Willamette Valley who knows about Elgin, since I was once the minister at the Elgin United Methodist Church. Furthermore, I teach an experiential form of psychotherapy, Hakomi Therapy, that requires a high level of personal and professional integration. She likewise likes to teach philosophy best by keying off narrative ac-

---

[2] Chairman of the Board of the Hakomi Institute, and United Methodist minister, retired. Dr. Johanson has taught adjunct at a number of universities, and been active in publishing, including, lead author (with Kurtz) of *Grace Unfolding: Psychotherapy in the Spirit of the Tao-te ching* (Bell Tower, 1991); and editor (with Weiss and Monda) of *Hakomi Mindfulness-Centered Somatic Psychotherapy: A Comprehensive Guide to Theory and Practice* (Norton: 2015).

counts, poetry, and art work. This volume that includes many of her short stories and poems followed by intellectual reflections embodies this integrative bias.

We are delighted enough with our contact that I accept an offer to join her in some monthly meetings in her care facility with other retired professors who travel to attend. Over several seasons of personal and intellectual sharing I'm familiar enough with her work that I suggest putting together the present volume.

I have taken initiative in assembling and organizing the book's materials because Pat is in a care facility due to an unusual form of Parkinson's disease that does not allow her to use paper and pencil, a keyboard, or voice-activated recorders. She is an example of mature people one meets in senior facilities whose bodies are failing them, whose verbal communications can be strained, but whose minds are still passionately alive, and able to run IBM, General Motors, teach philosophy, or dissect current events.

It is appropriate to say more of Pat's personal story since her personhood feeds so substantially into her academic work. She was raised in Elgin, Oregon on a ranch where she rode horses and did all the labor associated with a working home-farm, while experiencing life in a rural community. She married a local guy with whom she had four children. He turns out to be troubled, and subsequently abusive. She does not yet have a strong sense of who she is or what can be done in her situation. Around 30 she has a bout of tetanus that nearly kills her, followed by complications of fibromyalgia, tendinitis, jaw and shoulder surgery that ultimately prevent her from doing full time work in subsequent years.

Then she experienced what the literature would describe as a mystical occurrence, accompanied by energy, light, peace, colors, images, and a strong wisdom that communicated to her that people should never be less or more than what they are. This unique strength allowed her to divorce her husband, though she hurt for his predicament. It sustained her through many years of being a single mother with the singular aim of successfully sustaining and launching her children with little income.

When the kids progressed with a strong showing and were doing well, she eventually turned toward more formal education for herself. Though no one had ever encouraged her as smart, she had already been doing serious home studies on her own. In theological terms it could be said she went off to higher education with "faith in search of understanding." She studied both deeply and widely at Eastern Oregon State College, Mt. Angel Seminary, Oregon State, the University of Oregon, and Marylhurst College.

"Faith in search of understanding," is a crucial phrase for appreciating how Pat studied, and how the eventual Professor Herron taught and wrote. She is a throwback to old philosophers who believed that philosophical concepts had a relationship to life. She had experiential referents for the abstract concepts she encountered. In her reading she would compare her experience with those of the authors, a superb live way to study. In her writing she would feel that she was having conversations with peers about real experiences in the world as they were explored through the classic thinkers.

This approach, of course, is not understandable to many contemporary philosophers who deal more strictly with issues of language and epistemology. While Pat is debating the nuances of the known, many of her contemporaries are debating what one can really know, or how one can know? While she studied Wittgenstein and other post-structural writers such as Derrida who affirm that everything is known contextually, and thus, nothing can have an absolute finality or completeness, she was not willing to live at this level of meta-analysis forever.

She sided more with theorists such as Wilber (1995) who affirm that though the system is contextual and sliding, it does not mean that meaning can't be established, that truth doesn't exist, or that contexts won't hold still long enough to make a simple point. She joins with those who criticize the postmodern self as de-privileged and caught in despair, swallowed up in a social construct of signs and roles without hope, at the mercy of its own conscious and unconscious power interests, with no center as every meaning is deferred and erased in an ever-shifting flux of contexts. As such, according to Cornell West (1985), postmodernism provides no basis or criteria for authentic living or social reform.

8

Robert Torrance (1994) argues that the human species may be designated *animal quaerens* with at least as much right as *animal rationale*. More specifically, the human quest is in the service of self-transcendence or expanded consciousness. This translates that humans are animals that quest for the spiritual. The quest is wide-spread and broadly conceived. Religion as process is one source of the spiritual quest. But if the human being is truly *animal quarens*, a similar latency will be found in the biological, psychological, and linguistic conditions of human life and culture without which society and religion would themselves be inconceivable.

Patricia Herron is an existentialist who believes that life is an act that occurs in the midst of concrete, historical, passionate experience; that self-transcendence must never abstractly leave behind. The earthiness of her life and work with its foundations in eastern Oregon show up in her dramatic, raw, no-nonsense stories. They and her poems often provide helpful reference points as she reflects, in dialogue with the philosophical tradition on abstract categories that for her have experiential referents.

*Earthy Existentialism* is a rare category-busting book that combines life stories; experience-based, wise reflection; and poetic expression.

**References:**

Torrence, Robert M. (1994). *The Spiritual Quest: Transcendence in Myth, Religion, and Science.* Berkeley: Univ. of California Press.

West, Cornel (1985). "Afterword," in J. Rajchman and C. West, (Eds.) *Post-Analytic Philosophy.* New York: Columbia Univ. Press.

Wilber, Ken (1995). *Sex, Ecology, Spirituality: The Spirit of Evolution.* Boston: Shambhala.

# *Poems* & Prose

*The poems in this volume were written from 1972 to 1976. The house was located on Indian Creek three miles from Elgin, Oregon. It was in this home that I raised my four children, Wayne, Brian, Glen and Lynn Ann, and continued to meet and know the disguised characters in the short stories below.*

*These poems had been tucked away for years until the fall of 2002 when I shared "The Tiny, Yellow, Buttercups" poem with a close friend, and also read it to my Near East Religion class. It was then that I decided to resurrect some of these early poems. I was reluctant to do so as I am not a poet by nature. However, many changes and new insights were occurring at that time in my life. Poetry seemed the natural way for me to express these new realities. They offer the poetic expression of the earthy prose of the short stories of Eastern Oregon that follow.*

## The Bird on the Bed

Once I woke up in the night and saw a bird there by my
    side.
I said to the bird, "Who are you? What do you want? What
    can I do for you?"
"Don't be fooled by the world," it said, "do whatever it is you
    do . . . whatever that is".
I think to myself, with the bird there beside myself.
"It's not what you think," the bird said, turning itself around
    and around.
"It is much more than what you think, it is much, much
    more indeed.
It is a whole life and yourself, that will be turned around,
    and upside down,"
The bird then flew up and then down,
And around and around
And then out.

# For the Good of Mazie

As Mazie walked toward home, the dark clouds suddenly wrapped themselves around the full moon. Its light was dimmed but not obliterated and the darkness became alive as if with a strengthful purpose. The light penetrated and darted across the face of each cloud.

Mazie's long strides were interrupted as she paused and drew in her breath for a lengthy stare at the unexpected illumination. She felt she was being lifted upward, as though her soul wanted to join the clouds. Feeling compelled to break the spell, she bent over and picked up a pebble and threw it at what seemed to be the shadow of a man standing beside a huge oak tree. The rock spun through the illusion and landed alongside Ainsworth's old shed that was full of leftover chickens.

When Mazie saw where the small stone had come to rest, she smiled a half grimace as she remembered watching the two white roosters strut about their pen. At times they would ruffle their feathers and stretch their necks out as if preparing for a showdown. "They could fight, I'm sure of it," she thought, as she continued her walk until she came to the Ainsworth's lane that was lined with a few scraggly cottonwood trees, two lopsided yellow willows, and four really sick lilac bushes. The night shadows skipped through the trees giving them an illusion of splendor. It was early Spring and the tree limbs were awakening with tiny swellings, the new buds opulent, unaware of their lopsided and scraggly destiny.

Mazie looked down at her new blue tennis shoes and was disappointed to see that the blue now appeared gray. She loved new things and enjoyed these greening trees.

"Why not take them roosters to the cock fights?" she thought with a frown, as she contemplated the now not-so-new looking tennis shoes. She kicked at a large rock that suddenly appeared in her path. "I know about them cock fights, they've been going on for years and no one ever gets arrested even though it is agin' the law." She felt a quick surge of pain in her toes and foot. "It sure wasn't too smart of me to kick that rock, but it is outa the way now." A sad grimace darted quickly across her face.

She looked at her hands covered with cotton gloves she wore almost until the Fourth of July, as her hands were unusually sensitive to cold weather.

"Yes," she thought, "Ole Ted Sommers has those fightin' roosters. Tomorrow morning I've got to take my welfare check to town. I'll just stop by and tell him I have now some chickens and I plan to fight 'um."

Mazie's steps seemed lighter as she walked past the ailing lilac bushes. She now had a project, and a forbidden one at that,

She turned now as she entered Ainsworth's house and glanced out of the window as if she had been indoors for days. Mazie loved her new short span-of-time home. She would polish and clean until the house fairly sparkled, especially the windows, as she could see far and wide through these invisible intruders.

She walked to the Earth Stove and tossed in a log. She then took two long steps and sunk into a huge easy chair. She hadn't removed her gloves, a strange habit of hers. She sometimes forgot and other times she kept them on purposely.

Suddenly she was startled out of her peace by a loud knock that rang through the house like a sliver entering the skin, making Mazie shiver. She looked toward the door, evidently not remembering about knocks, not remembering at all.

Rosie Good finally opened the door and shouted, "Hey, Mazie:"

"I don't know who you are," Mazie said,

"Remember, I am Rosie Good from the church. I promised Father to look in on you every day."

Mazie still couldn't remember, and her power of speech seemed to have been misplaced.

"Ros-ie Go-od---I don't know---I don't know any Ros-ie Go-od, but I do remember the Goo-od," Mazie said.

"Yes, Mazie, I suppose you can remember the good," she said, half to herself, thinking what a pathetic creature Mazie really was.

The chair in which she sat seemed to engulf Mazie's girlish figure. Her face resembled a painting that hung near the main altar in the church. It depicted an angel hovering over an earthly scene, the angel's face neither belonging to earth nor heaven.

This awkward comparison always haunted Rosie. She now saw both the picture and Mazie, and also noticed that Mazie's hair

16

had become very grey. Rosie stared at this incongruity, grey hair on such a cryptic face. She knew that if she were to dye her daughter's doll's hair grey, it would compare admirably with Mazie's.

Rosie ignored Mazie and started to move about the house. While in the kitchen she moved the fry pan from the stove to the sink and, turning on the hot water faucet, filled it with water. "Let this pan soak for awhile, Mazie, and don't let the water down the sink as it has grease in it."

Mazie stared at Rosie as if she didn't exist. Rosie stared back, then quickly finished her inspection. Mazie's mood made her feel uneasy.

"Remember to put another log in before bedtime, Mazie, or you'll be cold before morning. I'll be back tomorrow," she added, as she went out the door.

Mazie remembered who Rosie was now and she smiled her sad grimace at her. She also remembered tomorrow as she snuggled deeper into the chair, planning every detail.

Mazie seemed to be an ageless person. When she was 25 she looked to be 45 and now that she was 53 she still looked 45.

Life hadn't been kind to Mazie. She had fallen into a dry well when she was 21, just before she was to marry John O'Brian. She had been unconscious for 6 months, John had married her best friend, Joanne, and Mazie was left with brain damage. This affected her memory. At times she did quite well and at other times she seemed to have complete memory loss. As she had grown accustomed to her handicap, she would compensate for her memory loss by listening to the TV, radio, or the conversations of others until something would be said that would help her recall where she had left off.

Following the accident her sincere parents provided money for therapy and physical support. But she had three brothers and five sisters and the parents finally decided that for the good of the other family members they could no longer provide for Mazie. Three of the other children wanted to attend college, and with all the other expenses for a large family, further expenditure was impossible. They passed her like a hot plate of baked beans to the State.

It was then decided by social workers with the help of a competent psychologist, who gave Mazie a series of tests, that she

17

was incurable. The psychologist had a funny habit of rubbing his chin with the back of his hand. He also had black eyes, one of which was slightly crossed and with an inclination to look at the side of his nose. He had rubbed his chin and said, "I feel that Mazie's condition is such that for the good of the State we cannot invest money in her for rehabilitation. She cannot be helped. She is, however, capable of menial labor."

As Mazie was Catholic, the parish priest in Elkton was also summoned. For the good of the church, Mazie would of course remain a member, but only a child member, as she couldn't remember most of the dogma. The church there even gave her a job as church caretaker, and she did any and all jobs that the adult members thought up to help her be responsible. She was also paid $150.00 a month by them, and the public welfare matched this amount. She was now set up for life, and for the good of her family, her country, and her church she lived in the church basement where there were exposed furnace pipes on the ceiling and only one small window. Directly on the outside of this infinitesimal 'apartment' stems of large rose bushes could be seen. The roses, of course, bloomed higher up and were out of her view.

Mazie slept in the chair until early morning. The huge white roosters were responding to the new day with loud, shrill "cock-a-doodle-do's." Hearing their crowing she remembered what she had planned for her day and jumped from her sanctuary. Her hands were cold even with the gloves and her body shook. She opened the stove door and looked at the gray, cold ashes. In the corner of the stove she saw a piece of log that was still alive with tiny red spots along one side. Mazie gathered some small chips in a paper sack near the stove and with a piece of paper she placed them gently over the tiny red coals. The smoke began to curl upward, slowly penetrating the interior of the stove and then, with sudden illumination the paper burst into flame and all became one as it slowly burned.

Mazie enjoyed starting fires and, unknown to others, she had, at times, intentionally forgotten to put the log on the fire in the evening. She now placed some larger chips and a small log on the burning area and, leaving open the draft, she swiftly turned toward the kitchen. She was too excited about the visit to Ted's home to eat her usual hot breakfast. She hurriedly ate two pieces of toast and grabbed a banana to eat along the way.

Mazie rode along, feeling the cold breeze whip against her face.. Her legs were tired already and she could feel surges of pain beginning in her feet and moving upward. She had to push hard to turn the large wheels of her old bicycle. The three miles to Ted's home seemed much longer for her than her usual jaunts.

The gloves still snuggled her hands and a bright yellow and red scarf covered her head. Her old brown coat and faded blue jeans seemed incongruent in contrast. As she passed the Higgins place, Old Lady Higgins was watching from the window. She turned to her husband who was putting on his farm boots, and said, "Why would anyone in their right mind wear such a bright scarf with an old coat?"

"Can't see wheres its any of your damn business, you old busy-body," he growled in reply as he stood to leave, thinking about the childlike trust Mazie had in all creatures.

He had always been attracted to Mazie. She seemed to possess an innocent beauty that intermingled with his ideal of a perfect woman. He wondered at times if she would still have this off-beat charm if she were normal. He now thought of the bright scarf as Mazie's innocence where a trace of true radiance existed.

A cat rubbed against his leg. He kicked and cursed at it and wished his wife could wrap something bright around her personality. He then swung toward the cow shed where a spotted milk cow was due to give birth.

Mazie walked into Elkton's First State Bank. She went up the narrow entrance way and then turned in the direction of the cashier's window. She paused momentarily and reached her gloved hand up toward the bright colored scarf. "How different it is," she thought, "from the hair of the ladies behind the windows." She smoothed her short bangs down, wondering how she would look with a fancy hairdo piled on top of her head. She glanced at her old jeans and frowned as she stepped to the window. Irma Gleason smiled her "Welcome to the bank" smile and barely opening her mouth, said, "Hello, Mazie, how are you today? Did you bring your check?"

"I brought it. Just a second, though, I have to fish it outa my backpocket." The welfare check had been folded into a small tight

19

square and was shoved into her hip pocket with various other treasures.

"Mazie, how many times must I tell you not to fold the check in so small a square? It's very difficult and time consuming to smooth it all out again."

"I can't remember you telling me all that. I don't carry a purse or nothin'. Besides, what are pockets for anyways?" Mazie said with a smile. Her grimace had disappeared.

As she went out the front door she noticed Tim Walker's old black and white cattle dog sitting on top of the pickup cab. He had moved up from his territory in the back of the rig and had his head held high as if he were on guard duty. Mazie realized that her memory was beginning to fail her. Just what was it she had planned?

A group of farmers was standing in front of Tim's pickup so Mazie stood close by in order to overhear their conversation.

"I still have that bottle of whiskey. I went down to the liquor store. Hadn't been there for years," Tim said.

"Guess we'll all come by and help you drink it. You have an old manure spreader out there don't you? I need one." another man spoke.

"I have a manure pile if you want it and I'll even throw in some dead lambs," replied a man smoking a pipe.

"Say, if you tie a big bulldog to your fence you won't need electric fences," spoke a large man with a laugh. "By the way, I'm ready to pour the slab for my new stove, If any of you run into an old hub of a wheel, I can use it when I pour the concrete as I can get an outline of the wheel for a design."

"Did you see Tuttle's old plow sitting out there after the old storage shed burned? Old Tuttle had been waiting 20 years for that fire."

"Are you going to get them tonight?"

"Yes, tonight's the night."

Suddenly Mazie remembered. "Yep," she thought, "today is the day and I must go on to Ted's and talk him into taking me to the cock fights.

Mazie wasn't shy about knocking on doors. Sshe doubled her gloved hand into a tight fist and pounded as though the door were the lifeless world. She paused, and straining her ears, heard movements from within. But she continued to bang.

Ted Sommers opened the paneled door. Just then Mazie was giving it her best bang. Her gloved fist flew through the open space and almost struck Ted in the chest. He glared at her, a deep crimson color creeping up his neck and slowly covering his face. Mazie stood and watched this ascent with interest, not understanding the full impact of his feelings until he screamed at her.

"What's all the pounding about? I heard you the first time." Mazie cast her blue eyes downward and thought, Why is he talking about pounding? Did I do something wrong?

Then it became clear that her knocks had been a series of loud thumps. She never knew that sometimes her actions were extreme unless someone told her. She stood exposed with this realization, like a nude person who has just been sprayed with water. How she hated these embarrassing moments. Raising her head she stared at him pleadingly, much like a hungry lost child.

The crimson slowly disappeared from Ted's face and then he in' turn, felt awkward. Overly enthusiastically he invited Mazie in.

She had her choice of chairs, overstuffed easy chairs, straight-backed, straight-backed wooden one. She chose the latter as she was on business and business meant seriousness. She sat there as stiff as an old maid at a poker game, and then blurted out, "I'm interested in the cock fights."

"What in the world do you mean, Mazie? You ain't got any cocks."

"I now have some roosters. I'm taking care of the Ainsworth's place while they are working for a spell in Pine Grove, and they have a bunch of chickens."

"So, you do have some roosters, huh?"

"I want to know where the fights are."

"Cock fighters aren't ordinary roosters, Mazie."

"Mine are big ones. They are always actin' as though they would like to fight."

"But, Mazie, cocks are bred and trained as fighters. And we use sharp spurs on their feet."

"Well, I sure wouldn't put any such things on my roosters' feet. But I bet they could fight if one was to give them half a chance."

21

"Mazie, why don't you come tomorrow afternoon and just watch."

"Well, I might, but where is it?"

"My south field around 1:00 o'clock. You know the field in back of the barn. You mustn't tell anyone and for God's sake, don't bring your roosters. You can't fight 'um anyhow.." Ted felt his generous invitation had discouraged Mazie. She could come, but no roosters. Just the thought made him cringe.

After her long ride home, Mazie went to the large back room in the Ainsworth house and chose a huge cardboard box. It was just the right size, as two roosters could fit into its narrow quarters. She picked it up and, taking a screwdriver from the shelf, she made little holes at random on the sides. "Tomorrow will soon be here," she thought as she heard Rosie's knock.

This time she remembered about knocks. She also remembered the log and had even removed her gloves before going to bed. Early next morning she put them on again before picking up the box. She was eager to get started.

Mazie placed the box beside the chicken house and went inside the pen to catch the roosters. They flew in all directions, stirring up the dust until Mazie had to fan the air with her gloved hand in order to see. The task seemed impossible. The sounds of their squawking and hundreds of small feathers filled the dusty, smelly air. But Mazie was determined and finally managed to grab one rooster and then another by a leg, after the time spent in the chase finally exhausted them.

Mazie was also exhausted and she sat for awhile wiping the sweat and dirt from her face with a red and white handkerchief. She then rigged up an old wagon with a rope and after tying it on the shaft beneath the seat of her bicycle she was off. The going was awfully slow, as the wagon and chickens added even more weight for her legs to pull.

Mrs. Higgins was in the yard spreading some garbage scraps on her flower beds and then folding them into the rich, black soil. She saw Mazie and stood and stared at her while leaning on her shovel. She couldn't suppress her laughter as the wagon pulled Mazie and her bike first one way and then the other. Sweat was pouring down Mazie's face and remaining in spite of the wind. She would wipe it off quickly with her gloved hand, only to have it replaced by more. Mrs. Higgins' laughter penetrated Mazie causing the sad grimace to reappear.

Ted Sommers saw Mazie zigzagging across the field. She was only about 20 yards from the gathering when he saw that the box had air holes. He didn't laugh, as he knew what it contained,

"By damn, she brought those roosters," he shouted, His voice was not heard as Mazie was late and the second fight was just beginning. Two dead cocks, covered with blood, were heaped in a pile a short distance from the pit which was fenced in with chicken wire.

Mazie parked her entourage nearby and rushed over to the ring. She saw two men in the center of the ring, each holding a cock. These men moved the heads of the fowl close together until they began to peck at each other. From the remarks she heard Mazie gathered that this was to get them in a fighting mood. The men then placed the birds in opposite corners, holding on to them with both hands. The referee entered the pit and began a slow countdown. "Five, six, seven, eight, nine and ten. Pit your chickens."

Mazie stood at the far end of the pit watching intently as the referee uttered the numbers. Her face was flushed with excitement and she was possessed with some of the strong feelings of the other spectators. As Mazie looked around her she thought their faces resembled the ugly masks she hated so much at Hallowe'en.

At the command the men picked up the cocks and threw them toward the center of the pit. The birds flew in with their feet aimed at each other. Two-inch long spurs were attached to the legs of the chickens. They jabbed at each other with these spikes until their fury became frenzy. The smallest of the two was finally flung down as the long spur from the foot of the other was stuck in his head.

Mazie stared at this arena of death with eyes that seemed spun backward in terror. She was as a person in a trance. The sweat ran down her face and her only movement was to raise her gloved hand occasionally across her dirt-streaked face. She had forgotten her red and white handkerchief.

The referee stopped the fighting long enough to pull out the spur. Since the cock was still alive, the fight continued until it was down but not yet dead.

"If the owner can revive him in 20 seconds he can reenter the fight." The victor this time was given one point. He still needed two more points in order to win.

Blood was streaming down the smaller chicken's head and spreading onto his body. The liquid made the feathers stick together in little red tufts.

Mazie watched the blood pour over the body and felt nauseated. The sweat pouring down her own face now became blood. She rubbed her face frantically and yet could not leave the scene. She could only stand and stare.

The owner picked up the broken piece of agony and began to blow on his head with the hot stale air from his mouth. He then held up his wings and blew under them. The cock's bloody head was still limp and it hung alongside his crumpled body. There were only five seconds left. His owner knew still another method for reviving the cock. He turned him upside down, blood dripping to the ground. The owner then blew air into the cock's rectum, causing its head to pop up and its body to jerk. The bird was ready to fight again.

The referee erased the gained point from the score sheet. Water was quickly poured over the bodies of the cocks, making them slick so the spurs couldn't enter so easily. The water ran down the back of the injured bird, changing its white feathers into a light pinkish red.

Mazie watched in disbelief. "What was happening?" she thought. " Perhaps they were cleaning him up and would then stop the horrible fight." She again ran her gloved hand over her face, then abruptly dropped the hand as if it were not attached to her arm as the count-down again rang out and the fight resumed. The pink red cock's courage was futile, and within a couple of minutes it was evident that he had been punctured in the lung as blood was flowing from its beak. He was also making a loud gurgling noise. It didn't have long to live but continued to try to fight as the referee didn't interfere.

Mazie watched the injured cock and suddenly forgot why she was at the fight. She looked at the crowd for a clue, and then moved over to where two men were talking...'

"That cock ain't got long to live."

"Ya, once the lung gets a poke it's goodbye Cock," the other man laughed out of the side of his mouth.

24

"Too darn bad too, I woulda like to seen that small one win." With the words "small one win" Mazie suddenly remembered. She had come to fight the roosters and she wanted them to win.

But now she was confused as she watched the cock's life ebb slowly away like a drowning man. He slowly jerked to the ground, his feet with the spurs pointing toward his owner. He then stretched his neck full length and died.

The spectators were now in some type of heightened ecstasy. Some were shouting to throw the dead cock aside so the next fight could begin. Bets were being collected and the owner of the dead bird gave $20 to the victor's owner.

Mazie was unable to reconcile these happenings. She hadn't known or prepared herself for such a bloody scene. She walked to the wagon. The roosters were huddled in a corner. Her only thought was to care for these forlorn creatures. She removed a small can of chicken feed from the wagon and started to place it through the holes in the box.

Doing this made her remember that she needed to buy some groceries. In her excitement of the last two days she had forgotten to stop at Elkton Foodland for her monthly food supply. She halted the feeding and reached into her back pocket and pulled out a small pad with a short stubby pencil attached along its top.

She stood beside the roosters, turning her head from side to side in an attempt to remember what she needed and as the items slowly came to her she carefully spelled out every other letter or so of each word. At this time a couple who owned and fought cocks noticed her.

"What in hell is that retard doing here?" Will Hadley shouted as anger roiled his round face like dark clouds surrounding the moon.

"How would I know?" his wife shouted in reply. "Leave her alone ·and go get 'Go Henny' ready to fight."

"But she's writing something on that pad. I tell you I don't like it!"

"O, don't bother her. Everyone knows she has problems. She probably dropped in by chance."

Will, who was short and stocky, couldn't be persuaded. He stormed over to where Mazie stood. His wife followed him as if he were pulling her along like a dog on a chain. He walked right into Mazie's space, standing only about three inches from her face. He was the same height as she so they were eye to eye.

25

Mazie jerked her head backward in surprise but would not move her feet from their position. Her gloved hand released the note pad, as she now felt the full shock of the situation. Feelings that she had been avoiding now flooded through her being like a dam released of its water. Why had she come to these bloody fights and what was this awful man doing staring at her so hatefully? Her body seemed to be filled with painful jerks.

"What are you doing here?" Will shouted, blowing hot air into her face.

"I came here to fight my roosters," Mazie said with her head held back, but her feet still firmly planted. At this remark the startled man looked into the box.

"Hell, those ain't nothin' but White Leghorn roosters. Those ain't fightin' cocks. You can't fight them."

It was apparent that his anger was now close to frenzy.

Mazie felt the flood again. She had been so determined, so very determined to get the roosters here and now she hated it all, the bloody cocks, the high pitched shreiks of the spectators, and now this hateful man who kept blowing his hot air into her face. She felt like the cock who had been revived by his master.

"You just try to fight them roosters and we'll see what will happen."

Mazie jerked alive. Her entire body was trembling and her gloved hands were shaking. She bent over and picked up her note pad and pencil.

"Oh, yes, I must not forget the salt. I've been out for weeks." She wrote SLT on the pad. Then she picked up her bike that was leaning against a pile of chicken wire and began to slowly pull the wagon and its cargo toward the ring.

The man ran beside her shouting, "You just try to fight them roosters."

His wife again followed closely. Mazie's entourage had certainly grown. The unlikely group reached the pit and the spectators had turned to watch. Some were pointing and laughing while others, like Will, were shouting with anger.

The deep crimson color crept quickly to the face of Ted Sommers. It was as if Mazie was pounding at his door. He was ready to grasp her by the arm, as she seemed about to open the box, her gloved hand:

rested on its top. She slowly turned toward her audience and spoke in a shaky voice.

"I had planned for days to bring my roosters here to fight, I thought--I thought it would be good, but it isn't good, is it? If you all don't mind, I'll just take them home and bury them."

She walked to where the dead birds were and, reaching out her gloved hands, she gently picked them up and placed them toward the front of the wagon. The sight of their dead brothers caused the roosters to huddle in the far corner of the box.

The crowd stared in silence as she mounted her bike for her journey home.

## *The Doe by the*
## *Side of the Road*

By the side of the road
Lies a doe
Struck by a fast-moving car.

As I pass this awesome sight
I feel a twinge of pain.

My thoughts quickly envisage the
Beautiful deer; running swiftly
Through the meadows.
Leaping with the grace of
Ballet dancers using space as their stage.
Creating splendor with their flowing
Sublimity of motion.

LIFE conquers the living, while death
Plays such a reverse in roles.

The County Road Department seems
Oblivious of the forgotten doe
Beside the road.
And she remains there day after day.

One night I dreamt as I passed her by,
That the breath of life was there
And reversed her plight, and oft she leaped
Into the sky, blending into
The stage of light.
LIFE, the conqueror of all that is.
Gathers up Death
And consumes it as it passes by.

(This poem was written in 1976 and of course the idea for the poem
was the fact that I did, indeed, pass a dead doe beside the country
road on Indian Creek.)

# Hand

A late April wind whines through the tall spruce and pine trees on the high Wallowa mountains in northeastern Oregon. The peaks and high ridges are covered with snow, as the wind denies the sun's warming comfort. Patches of snow cling to the lower slopes and ridges.

A seasoned wapiti cow walks slowly along a forest path, her head bent downward. The trail is covered with a soft springy duff of pine needles. A hawk's shriek shatters the quietness of the plodding trek.

Under a tall Ponderosa pine, the elk finds a soggy soft bed as her front hooves sink comfortably into the spongy moss. She awkwardly stretches her extended body onto the bed, She rests awhile. The time has arrived. Snorting, her body begins to heave and strain, her breath gasps in and out, as the life in her womb pushes frantically against her sides. Deep jabs of pain rhythmically bounce through her and she emits loud eerie squeals. Her body is being jerked apart, tearing and pulling as though two mighty hands have reached down onto the forest floor.

Suddenly the pulling hands release their brutal grip, and with a deep intake of air she pushes until a wet, ugly, bloody head emerges. Again and again the cow strains. The head slips out of the birth canal followed by a damp, slick body with stick-like legs pressed to its sides. A slimy substance clings to the new body as though to protect the curled heap a second or two longer.

The heap is a bull calf. His lungs expand and expel his first breaths, but the new elk is unaware of this life force. Roselike he exists only in being.

The cow uses her long rough tongue to cleanse, caressing until the birth film is removed. The fur reacts and as it dries, it springs upward like tiny sprouts emerging from the soil.

Spindly legs begin to jerk, as the awakening head lifts into life. Kneeling awkwardly on his two front legs, the calf slowly moves his rump up with the two rear sticks. He sways gently back and forth and it looks as if he will fall: He does. But after struggling, falling, and finally gaining control, he stands and wobbles a couple of feet to where the sun's rays momentarily touch the damp earth.

A black crow sweeps gracefully onto an air current. His flight paints a shadow across the tree tops and touching the forest floor it passes briefly over the new bull's back and sides.

The young elk begins to stretch and jerk his head about. The cow moves close to him and the tiny nose and mouth butt against her tender belly. His soft muzzle touches the udder and within a few seconds his mouth surrounds a teat. He sucks, awakening to the cow's smell and the warm liquid rushing into his body.

The calf is tawny brown, and darker on the face, belly, neck and legs. A large buffy rump patch surrounds a bobbed tail. The darker color on the face is shaded with a patch of light fur resembling a man's outstretched hand. The empty hand reaches out like the mysterious force ebbing in and out, sweeping across the sky with the winds, crawling along the forest floor with the insects, passing over all animals large or small. The gigantic hand gently caresses the young suckling fastened securely to the warm soft teat. The youngster butts against the udder and grabs onto another long slick lifeline. The sucking sounds dance playfully with the wind, and the new little belly stretches with warm milk, The calf is satisfied now and exhausted. He slumps forward and falls again into the birth heap.'

H i s first birthday departs as dark shadows dart through the forest. The trees seem to gather together like a fortress to reject the light. The mother moves to her sleeping son as she feels an unspeakable concern.

Large gray timber wolves start their low mournful howls. Certain sounds can freeze the blood and the shrill, pitched yelps and wails of wolves late at night are among them.

The cries echo against the high ridges and bounce among the trees as though everything is endowed with language.

These lamentations communicate fear in the seasoned cow, Memories surface of sharp teeth teasing the flesh of an old cow. The winter had been longer and colder than usual. Many old cows and bulls, as well as the weak yearling calves had been slaughtered. The green eyes of the wolves had stared through the trees before they charged, and then their ugly fangs had dripped with fresh blood. The cow remembered that sweet obnoxious odor as shivers of instinctive fear envelope her. Reaching, she nuzzles the calf gently. A mouse scurries over the youngster's back and thigh and disappears into his underground home. It too feels the violence of the eerie language.

Morning arrives. The calf struggles to stand, and his efforts are easier. The sticks have become supporting legs, legs that can bend back and forth, legs that move him around in order for him to find the warm udder. He recognizes the care, security and food offered by the large object. He discerns the object's odor and also discovers that he can chirp, a squealing little whine that is almost birdlike. And the creature next to him chirps in response, which will, in the future, be used to call him. He is aware of being alive. He knows very little, but enough to survive right now.

The weeks pass and the calf grows stronger he enjoys following his mother on treks to the meadow where he can stray and romp until the cow chirps in low whines, signaling him to return to her side.

In late May cows and calves gather into small herds in search of high mountain ranges.

Before pioneers settled the west, elk were plains animals, much like the antelope and buffalo of the era. As humans tamed the West, however, the elk took to the remote regions of the most rugged mountains around.

The cow and calf now wait with the others before crossing the formidable Spoken River. The name had belonged to a famous Nez Perce Indian who had been the tribe's medicine man. Spoken River stood beside the river listening to its spirit before performing his sacred duties. The Indians believe that his spirit is now part of the river, waiting, always waiting, for quiet listeners.

The narrow trail leading to the river was surrounded by thick underbrush and towering trees. The herd moves slowly along before reaching a clearing on the bank, selected years hence as the place where the elk would ford Spoken River. The calves have to rest and nurse, and the cows patiently wait as their youngsters clung to their udders.

The boss is a big matriarch. She is the undisputed leader and controls the major movements of the herd. If the lead cow stops moving to feed or to bed, the entire herd stops. Her calf butts and moves from the udder; she can now prepare to cross. She steps into the icy water and drinks. Her large bull calf follows, wading out ahead of her. She angrily shoves him back. She is not ready and instinctively feels death swirling and churning, pushing violently against the bank, raging against it-self, as though each water droplet is struggling to finish first in the eternal race, on and on, never stopping to rest, going nowhere, yet everywhere.

She again butts her frisky calf and, stepping onto shore, she extends her huge head upward; she is like a person reaching for courage before a battle. The leader then lowers her head and turns quickly toward the herd, emitting a bark, a raspy woofing snort, as a sign of a possible but not certain danger. Waiting to assure that the herd was alerted, she then edges into the river.

She maneuvers her calf close to her side, away from the initial onslaught. The herd follows, pressing into one protective body, and like their leader they seek the safest positions for their young. One misguided step into a crevice or a fall could prove fatal and give the water a chance to sweep them over, folding and pulling them downward into the rushing undercurrent.

The new calf's mother took her allotted position near the outside rear. Although there is protection from the water's full force, they were vulnerable if the cow should trip.

There was no discernible communication but they all sensed danger near the outside rear. They cannot shout and shove as humans do. No, they follow the lead cow quietly, without fanfare or calculation, and merge and move forward as their positions on the bank unfolds like the constant flowing hydrogen and oxygen atoms uniting to create water molecules.

The moving body is almost to shore when an old barren cow, who had forgotten to die during the winter, suddenly slips. She is sandwiched into the middle of the Group, the waters immediately grabbing her and sweeping over her existence. The cows directly in her path quickly move aside, shielding their calves from her violent struggles. She wildly thrusts herself forward, striking out against the terrible foe. But the river holds her tight, and unable

32

to gain footing she collides with the bull calf's mother. The two cows are caught in a terrible death struggle.

A loud, raspy bark from the matriarch echoes through the herd, and the calf's mother whines pitifully as though calling to her calf, reassuring him.

The youngster has been shoved toward the shore escaping the strong current, but he is separated from the Group, as they are now climbing into the shore. The leader shakes the water from her legs and sides, her calf does the same. Feeling the water for the first time adds another dimension to his young forming life.

The young calf's first water experience grabs out with long gnarled fingers to pull him under-under-destroying, obliterating.

A few cows sniff the air and paw the ground as the weak squeals of the calf are lost in the river's roar, as the rushing waters try to pull him into the same turbulent grave as his mother. He fights courageously like a tiger in a hole trap, who runs up the dirt walls again and again, refusing to admit defeat.

The calf instinctively wants to live. His frantic kicking struggles move him along and toward the shore, finally thrust--ing him onto a small secluded beach surrounded on all sides by steep banks. It is as though Fate had decreed in advance that this beach would save the bull calf.

He lies exhausted, heart beating wildly, and gradually sinks into oblivion, becoming one with the stones and pebbles. Several hours later he awakes refreshed and rested but with a nagging hungry pang swirling through him with a strong even grip. He is eager to find his mother and her warm comfort to satisfy the tight empty feeling.

He staggers to his feet and slowly walks along the bank, not knowing that his mother now belongs to the river. He trudges on even after it feels that all life energy has been extinguished. It's like the flickering of a tiny flame that continues to exist only with the aid of some ancient spark deep within, like the hand stretching across his forehead, empty and forlorn.

Afternoon merges into evening twilight, shadows dance across the land frolicking with the calf's shadow, more alive than the animal who falters and falls, denying the shadows their dance. One illusion escapes, then reappears alongside the body heap, patiently awaiting his return.

A logging road is located near the spot where the young calf lies and soon a four-wheel drive pickup appears. The riders are two men wrapped in heavy logging clothes— baggy dirty pants held up by wide ugly suspenders, old faded red flannel shirts adding a touch of color.  Black mud-covered boots that are coldly drab. Their slogan advertisement hats shout out like neon sign 'Get Happy-Try Snappy John's on the cap of the driver and the passenger's cap joins in with 'Napa Auto Parts'. Lee is the name of the latter. He is called "Sorry" at times by the fellows as he seems to have worse luck than a porcupine chasing its tail.

His companion, Ike, has a more positive attitude, along with a firm opinion on every subject. Only two days ago Ike had exclaimed that the fish hatcheries located on Spoken River be eliminated, or as he would say "be done away with", as they are a waste of taxpayers' monies. His reasoning was unclear, but he was positive that fish could fend for themselves, hadn't they been doing so for years?  On and on Ike would talk on subjects he knew very little about. He talked as the bumped along.

"Those damn Forest Service guys steal the road maintenance money for the big shots' beer parties." Lee didn't answer.  He knew Ike talked mostly for his own enjoyment.

The road was rough and it irritated him also, especially fol- lowing a hard day at work. Maybe Ike was right; maybe the big shots did use the money for their beer parties.

"Hey, stop," Lee blurted as he caught a glimpse of the elk calf not far from the road. "I think there's an animal of some kind near that pine."

He shrugged, still talking. He wasn't about to give up his ongoing opinion without a struggle.

"Come on, stop, Ike, there's something there, I tell ya."

"O.K., O.K.," Ike said, placing his muddy boot on the brake. "But what are ya ranting and raving about? I don't see a thing."

"Over there, under the pine. It looks like a young deer or elk calf."

"Say, you're right," Ike replied, "and the cows are moving up high. Wonder where his mom is?"

The two men quickly stepped from the vehicle eager for a

closer look. The loggers enjoyed watching the animals as it broke the monotony of their long tedious days.

"He looks more dead than alive. His mother's met with a mishap for damn sure," Ike said in an offhand manner.

"Appears we'll have to take him to town and call the Forest Service," Lee responded. "You know the rules, it's against the law to keep orphaned animals, especially elk and deer. And besides what can we do for him? We don't have time to monkey with him."

Ike's long pointed chin jerked out.

"Christ alive, we can't turn him over to The Forest Service. Haven't you heard?"

"No, I ain't heard nothing and I doubt if you have."

"It's a fact. Sure, they feed them all right, and then cart them off to the zoo."

"A fact, you say. What's a fact anyways-hearsay, that's all."

"A fact, I tell you, straight from the mouth of ole Jake Edwards. His nephew, Mike, works on the clean-up crew for them Forest Service dudes up near Angleworm Creek."

Lee knelt and touched the trembling young calf, stroking its fur gently and speaking soothingly to it. "Aaaah."

"Appears you might be right. After all, Jake's nephew should know wheres he's working with them. This little fellow's pretty near dead. We've got to take him along."

"You're right. Here help me and we'll carry 'im to the rig."

The men carried the youngster to the pick-up. The young elk was too exhausted to fight. His only reaction was to stiffen and then jerk with his hind legs. They laid him on the pick-up bed next to the cab and covered him with some old gunny sacks.

As the pick-up rattled along, Lee would glance back occasionally,

"Ain't moved a muscle. Don't think he'll make it."

Ike didn't answer. He was too busy thinking and turning the sharp curve not far from the small farm belonging to D. James, also known as the Goat Man. D. James was an old recluse living off his few acres that nestled like an eagle's nest next to Indian Creek. Near the cabin was the goat shed and a small corral. Very few people in the quiet eastern Oregon logging community owned any goats.

The Goat Man was the target of numerous derogatory jokes, as nobody bothered to know him personally, for he didn't belong. He was a strange silent outsider. There were rumors that he was a World War I veteran and that he had at one time in his youth been a bronc rider.

"Say," Ike suddenly yelled, "Let's stop at the Goat Man's. Maybe he'll adopt him, and he'd have lots of milk for the little fella."

Lee nodded. "Sounds like a great idea to me. I sure don't know what else to do with him,"

They had given D. James a ride a few weeks ago. Ike had chattered along, but even the impact of his swift and terrible opinions didn't induce D. James to respond. He had only nodded his head every three minutes or so and had emitted a rough guttural sound deep in his throat. This had irritated Ike; he hated it when he couldn't get his listener fired up enough to at least make a comment.

As the two men walked up to the cabin Lee had misgivings.

"Let's forget it. The man's a bit crazy. He might shut the door in our faces or worse, just stare at us without talking. Remember the last time, the time we gave him that ride? He's real peculiar. Why, he might even eat the little guy."

"Eat who?  What the hell are you talking about? Haven't you heard the man is an animal lover and a vegetarian?" Ike growled through his tightly shut mouth as he reached for an old horse shoe hanging on the cabin door. He pounded a few times with the shoe as though striking out at his deaf and dumb listener.

Ike shook his head at Lee and then yelled at the door. "Come on D. James, it's cold out here. That wind never stops. Let us in."

The old man peered cautiously at them as he slowly opened the door. The two men stepped inside the crowded room and then stopped short. A huge eagle stared down at them. It must have had a wing spread of at least four feet, and it was perched on the mantle of the crude fireplace.

"My God, watch out!" Ike shouted. "That eagle's a'goin' to eat who? Eat us, that's who!

"Oh, For Chris' sake calm down. You don't have enough sense to pour pee outa your boot. He's stuffed. No live bird looks like that," Lee retorted.

"What say, you have pee in your boot? Why you comin' in here to tell me that?" D. James chimed in.

"No", Ike yelled, "I don't have any pee in my boot."

Ike then patiently explained about the bull elk calf. It was necessary to repeat the story as the old man repeatedly said, "What? What?" And finally, "Let me see him. A bull calf, orphan you say. Where's the cow? Did you shoot her?" D. James shouted excitedly, glaring at the men.

"Hell, no, we didn't shoot any cow out of season" Lee shouted back. "Come on, we'll show him to you:"

The calf lay in the rig, still confused by the strange odors. There was the oily smell of the machine mingled with the aroma of Ike's old shepherd dog who liked to lie on the gunny sacks. Where was the soft springy duff and smell of pine needles? His body shook. He wanted the comfort of the soft, slick teat and the familiar fragrance of his mother's body.

The two men watched silently as D. James allowed excitement to bring him out from his usual stoic self. The old man stared intently at the calf and then, stepping back, said, "I like him and he's a tough un'. Appears like he's been through a lot."

"We thought you might take care of him. We don't have time to monkey with him and the Forest Service jerks will send him to the zoo."

D. James rubbed his chin and spoke as if thinking aloud. "Well, now, come to think of it, one of my older goats lost her kids. Seems she's getting too old. Sure is a cranky ole gal."

And so it was settled. Three pairs of hands lifted and carried the youngster to the goat shed. Ike and Lee lingered awhile, not wanting to give up their prize. They reassured D. James they would stop by on Monday. The Goat Man didn't answer but was hoping they wouldn't. He was thinking about the elk, his thoughts racing ahead, planning how to care for him. He noticed the shape of a hand stretching across the bull's forehead.

"Guess I'll call you Hand," he said, stroking the image in the

37

fur. "How do you like that? Now rest awhile and I'll be back soon."

He then walked to the cabin and entering, he began to peek and peer into every corner. Papers, old magazines, and bits and pieces of all kinds of things cluttered every corner. He quickly threw everything into random heaps, as if searching for something. "It must be here somewheres. I don't remember tossing it out." He spoke aloud as he threw a pile of old newspaper into the fire. The flames leaped gleefully around the refuse as though welcoming it. D. James watched and then reached for a tin box on the mantle.

"Maybe it's in this old box," he said as he lifted the lid. And there it was partially hidden like the memories of his bull hunting days forty years or so ago.

He stared at it as though out of guilt and then softly spoke. "After the bloody war I never kilt another thing, not if I could help it." He felt the elk bugle call would make the young bull feel more at home.

The top hinge creaked and jerked as D. James opened the shed door, it needed oiling and it was also loose. He knelt, gently blowing the horn while rubbing the elk's silky fur. The young animal relaxed, and although the nagging hunger was now almost unbearable, his head raised and butted. The tongue licked air. The Goat Man placed his two middle fingers in the elk's mouth. Hand gripped tight and started to suck. But where was the warm liquid? Frustrated, he butted at D. James.

"Careful, boy, I'm not your mother but maybe I can find one for you.'"

He walked outside wiping his fingers on his upper pant leg. The old spotted she goat stood by herself in the corner of the corral. She pawed the ground, snorting and shaking her horns at D. James. Perhaps she resented in a way her monotonous life. Whatever the case, she was unhappy, and losing her twins had added to her anger.

D. James had named her Molly after a French girl he had slept with during the war. She had also been cantankerous, which had made making love to her virtually impossible. Especially since she had the tendency to flare up either before or after the climax. She seemed to have liked sex, and yet

38

resented it.

D. James' nerves soon couldn't take the extra strain. He wanted to leave the bloody warfare on the battlefield where it belonged, so when he couldn't placate the saucy mademoiselle, he had called it quits. The last time he had seen her she was talking vociferously to a battle-fatigued soldier whose look of bewilderment said plainly he had no idea what he had done.

D. James had then found another woman to quiet his desires, and another and then another until he soon realized they too were only looking for physical closeness and comfort, and that he had never loved anyone nor had anyone ever loved him. Just what was the big 'L' about anyway? He had often pondered it. But maybe, he had thought, there had been love between Grandmother Sarah and himself. Sarah had raised him after his mother had run off with Daniel W. Hamilton, the county tax adjustor. Everyone had hated Daniel as it seemed he was always snooping around raising the home owners' taxes. The citizens of Tex County couldn't even build a new out-house without Dan there on the spot inspecting and inspecting. One would think he thought he was God almighty and yet, strange to say, folks didn't hate the awesome inspecting God like they did Daniel.

Molly heartily resented her not on time inspector. What was he doing snooping around this time of day? He had milked her earlier. She turned around, kicking her tiny sharp hooves at him. "Get out - leave me alone," the swift kicks seemed to say.

D. James' gentle voice rang out, "Calm yourself. I ain't a-goin' to hurt you none. Come on back to the shed. I've something to show you." He kept talking, slowly and soothingly, moving in closer to her. She lowered her head until her curled beard was touching the ground, and then quickly raised it, ready for a charge to push him over the field and out of her life. Man and beast stared at each other, and then the man suddenly flung out his arms. "Come on, get to the barn. Enough of this foolishness."

The unexpected gesture broke Molly's stance and she whipped around toward the shed door, heels striking the air.

Once inside she stood still staring and sniffing at the strange object in the corner. The odor was familiar. She remembered smelling it in the meadow beside the creek. Large ugly animals gathered there briefly once a year. She wanted no part of this smell, none whatsoever.

She edged toward the far corner twisting her head downward, preparing for another charge; her left hoof pounded on the dirty board floor. Dust slowly rose around her until she looked like a phantom

D. James watched, fanning the air with his hands. It was hopeless. Molly was too cantankerous. He would have to feed the calf with a calf bottle or bucket.

And then suddenly Molly changed her mood. Her stiff body relaxed as she sniffed the air capturing impressions of the feeble Hand. She stood over him with what appeared to be a guard stand. She wanted him to recognize her smell.

D. James wasn't too surprised. He had lived too long close to nature and had seen many rare sights. Only two days ago he had seen a ground hog and a mouse play hide-and-seek. What a strange pair they were, running in and out amongst the rocks.

He watched quietly, not wanting to disturb the she-goat. Then, turning, he opened the door and stepped through the archway, reaching back with his right hand to softly and slowly close it and allow his idea to blossom. A smile of hopefulness cracked the crevices of his weather-beaten face. As he walked away, he whistled tunelessly to himself with great satisfaction.

The old man returned a half hour later and saw Hand standing and butting his head against Molly. He was desperately seeking the warm milk and since he was practically as tall as the old goat the task looked impossible. Grabbing onto Hand's head D. James gently moved it downward toward the udder. He needed to bend and stretch the head even further. Hand resented his help and jerked away. The Goat Man tried again and again until Hand's soft muzzle felt the warm teat. The young animal then lowered himself to his knees and eagerly began to suck.

He again felt the warm sensation trickling down his throat, spreading throughout his existence. But what a strange new mother, so small and such a strong, obnoxious odor: Not at all like his mother's comforting smell. He butted the bag and shook his head as if to dislodge the confusion. Drinking until he was full, he then sank to his knees and, stretching out on his straw bed and was soon asleep.

Molly refused to relinquish her mother role even after Hand was too large to nurse, and the Goat Man was feeding him from a bucket with a hard rubber nipple attached to the outside near the bottom. The maturing elk resented the coldness of the contraption at first, but the nagging hunger won out and he soon learned what would follow when D. James would appear beside the pasture gate. Upon finishing the eating, he would dart across the pasture to stand beside Molly, who would caress him tenderly. Even though he towered over his adopted mother, he still sought nurturing.

"Stop it, confound it," James yelled one morning during the feeding session. "You get more on your head than in your belly." He laughed as Hand continued to butt the bucket.

The lazy days of summer sped along for the threesome. D. James repeatedly blew the elk horn in hopes of preparing Hand for his return to the forest and his own kind.

One day in August the old man walked to the nearest ranch with a sack of his famous carrots tossed over his stooped shoulders.

Tilly Curtis opened their oversized front door when she heard the knock. Her large mouth and thick Lips twitched in surprise. Only rarely did D. James visit. "The last time," she thought, "must've have been five years ago when the creek was flooding due to the ice jam and he came to help."

"Why, hello, D. James. What a surprise! Real good to see you. What's in your sack?"

The old man reached into the sack and pulled out a giant carrot. Tilly knew about those carrots. She would stop by his place occasionally to see if he had extra ones for sale. They were much larger than average size and so succulent they would melt mysteriously in her mouth. How did he grow such jewels? No one knew.

"I would like to talk with Dale about trading them for something," D. James said.

"Why, sure, D. James, it would be nice to have some of your carrots. Dale's out back, behind the shed greasing up the tractor. Hurry and maybe you can catch him before he's gone to

41

the field."

Dale looked up, wiping his greasy hands on his overalls, as he was a habitual hand shaker.

"What can I do for you, D. James? It's been a long time."

"I would like to do some trading. These carrots" and he patted the sack, "for one of your cattle identification tags."

"Why, I guess so, but you can't use my number, it's against the law."

"I plan to scratch it out, and besides I don't want it for a calf."

"One of your goats then-huh?"

"Well, no, but I want one, just one for a special critter." Dale knew better than to inquire further. It would be easier to pull all the teeth out of one of his horses than to get more information from D. James.

"O.K., all right, but how's you goin' to put it in without the gun?"

"Thought maybe you could loan it to me for a spell. I'll bring it back later this afternoon."

Dale remained silent, rubbing his long, narrow chin. "I don't think so. I make it a point never to loan out equipment." He saw a look of disappointment swell up in D. James and a watery film seemed to wash across his steel blue eyes.

He relented. "O.K., just this once I'll do it. But have it back today."

D. James cringed. How he hated to ask for anything:

The old man walked home, feeling the sun's warmth penetrate his red cotton shirt. It felt good and gradually changed his mood. He felt as if he were the only person alive—just him and the dirt, rocks, grass and flowers soaking in the rays of the sun. But only D. James could feel the sweat trickle down his back.

Upon reaching home he went to his small work shop located off the main room of the cabin. Holding the metal tag in one hand he scratched off the numbers 627 that were printed across it. And with a tiny pick-like instrument used in leather work he proceeded with a slow steady hand, going over the fine letters again and again and finally there it was - G 0 A T-printed in bold letters. Grasping it and the gun-like tool in his right hand he walked to the corral. Hand had been waiting for the morning feeding, impatiently butting the fence.

"Hey, stop that. You'll bring down the fence. I'll soon have Molly milked."

Softly the milk flowed from the taut teats, capturing its own white upward-heaving froth. Splash, splash, softly, rhythmically the two white columns crossed and descended with a gentle swirling movement through the billowing foam.

Hand eagerly swallowed the warm meal, stopping once or twice to butt the bucket. Taking advantage of the young animal's absorption in food, D. James quickly moved his hand up Hand's neck toward the ear and, using the gun tool, pressed down through the small opening in the tag. The elk jerked his head swiftly upward, but the staple had entered the soft lumpy muscles and the tag was securely attached to the outside of the left ear. D. James hoped the tag would be a good luck charm against hunters and other mishaps.

Grandma Sarah used to tell him that if a body tamed and cared for a critter, they gave it a soul. So, if a hunter should kill Hand maybe he'd see that he was special.

"There, young fella, you now have some identification."

Molly and Hand hurried toward the opened corral gate and into the pasture. Hand shook his head as though a pesky barn fly had claimed his ear.

The tall aspen and willow trees growing along the creek swayed gently toward the two critters, reaching out to shelter them. The birds chirped loudly, fluttering and flapping, circling the pair.

Molly's smells were now second nature for Hand, but he remembered the odors of his first two weeks. And when he drank from the stream, he recalled the terror and struggle raging over him and pushing him down as if it singled him out for attack. D. James' elk call and these memories confused Hand. Was he a goat or a creature whose bellowing sounded like the low, guttural sounds coming forth from the man?

July eased into August like one long day. The time was near. D. James no longer fed Hand even though the angry elk had hung around the corral squealing in low pitiful undertones. He soon knew it was futile, that he would never again be

43

comforted with the warm milk. Never again would he run joyously, leaping and kicking toward the corral. No more would he feel the warm trickle slipping smoothly, caressingly down his long neck, the overspill oozing and foaming around his soft muzzle. Molly too sensed the change and began to strike her deadly hooves against the air as though preparing for the emptiness, a silent foe.

Toward the middle of September, a small group of elk cows and calves appeared in the meadow. Molly's nose sought the air and then sniffed at Hand. She forcefully shoved him toward the huge animals. D. James saw the intruders as the early morning light broke forth. He watched Hand's confusion. The young animal twisted as if in agony, first turning toward Molly and then in a meandering serpentine, reached the old matriarch of the elk herd.

He eyed and then sniffed her body. Then, like a contortionist, he moved again to Molly who watched, pawing the ground, striking and pounding. He tried to tease her, nipping and nudging, into a romp or a friendly race. She again pushed at him and turned away.

Hand stepped back, stark and alone. It was as if his mother, his comfort and security had changed into a creature with three dimensions, a grotesque combination of a goat, a man and an elk. But the pull was strongest in favor of the herd. Like the water had done, he was again being pulled away and toward a horizon not of his knowing. This time the struggle ended peacefully as he once again merged into the group. But the ghostly figure remained like a shadow creeping over his existence.

Molly turned, striking the air with swift kicks; the goat man raised his hand in farewell.

Rutting season followed by the yearly archery season had begun.

Hand quickly became accustomed to the habits of the herd. He was especially keenly aware of the mature bull who guarded his harem jealously. He would at times watch the bull copulate with one of the cows, until the two heaving, grunting beasts excited him to a frenzy. He would then move to a secluded spot, tear up the ground, urinate, and roll and toss violently on the wet dirt.

Young yearling bulls were allowed to remain with the herd as long as they didn't pose a threat. Hand's sordid act was the beginning urge that would soon make him a contender for the throne. The awesome battles would then begin, and loud sounds of elk bugling would sound off a warning to other bulls that a certain territory was being defended.

Archery season is deadly, taking place in the early fall while the vulnerable bulls are deeply involved in mating season.

One afternoon the herd was grazing on a wooded hillside when Hand heard a deep, guttural roar, the bugle call of a big bull challenging the herd bull. The old seasoned bull immediately jerked his head up in the direction of the sounds. The roar raced through Hand's memory, and with it, a brief recall of James and Molly. He sniffed as though hoping to capture the scent of the mixture of man and goat. His keen hearing detected the slight difference between a bugle call and the real bugling.

Hand watched the old bull react. He was rearing, snorting and pawing the ground, getting his enormous 1100pound frame ready to charge. He held his majestic body with dignity. Two antlers arose from large burrs high on the head, like long, bowed, cylindrical beams sweeping upward and backward over the shoulders. Attached to these beams were sweeping branches of tines.

The king responded to the bugle with a deep grunt and to demonstrate his confidence, he sprayed his belly with squirts of urine. He also let out three long, serial yelps, part of the urine spraying behavior. The old timer then charged down the hillside toward the intruder.

Hand followed eagerly, seeking adventure. The aged elk stopped and raked his antlers against a young spruce tree. This "horning" was yet another way of exhibiting confidence. He was like a knight decked out in shining armor, which assures victory.

Suddenly Hand heard a low, shrill sound intermingling briefly with the snorts and roars of the bull as he prepared for battle. And a familiar smell lingered in the air, the odor of man. Then the old bull crashed to the ground. Hand stopped, bewildered and frightened, as his nostrils flickered with the strange

45

fresh smell of blood.

He watched as the great bull moaned and kicked piteously upon the earth, all dignity gone. The arrow had pierced near the right side of the heart.  As he kicked into space with his long, slim legs it was as if he were space walking, charging toward his foe and victory. Invincibility lingered near. Faint snorts and gurgling sounds were heard as blood gushed out his nostrils and mouth. A human darted out from the thicket and quickly slit the bull's throat, the knife's long sleek blade flashing as though alive. The old timer stretched full length, jerked one last time and then sank peacefully onto the ground

An unknown fear overcame Hand, carrying the obnoxious blood and man odors as he raced away. Running, running, sweeping the limbs of the trees--not stopping until he was safe with the herd.

Hand was now in his nineteenth year. He is what the hunters describe as a 6X7, a trophy bull with six times on one antler-and seven on the other. He now weighs close to 1200 pounds. He gained much respect through the years and has acquired a large territory with many cows in his harem. Numerous scars attest to his many battles and narrow hunting escapes.

Once a year he guided his harem along the creek and meadow beside D. James' cabin. Molly has long since died, but the old man lingers on. As the herd quietly grazed, Hand would leave it briefly to stand on the knoll above the cabin to smell the familiar goat and human odors, remembering his early nurturing.

D. James had begun to expect the yearly visit and would respond with loud roars from the bugle. The elk would return with loud, snorting grunts, piercing the pre-dawn silence.

Hand's memories of the bugle call at the homestead were peaceful, but he remembered another bugle call, an old bull twisting in agony, and the man with the object gleaming and flashing. These events were coupled with the distasteful odor of blood. Hand, the new king, unable to arrange these experiences, they remained as a phantom, a ghost haunting and reckoning, beckoning to him.

On an evening following an overnight visit at the D. James

farm, the herd had moved to a low ridge a few miles away and were peacefully grazing on a well-timbered slope. Hand was calling to a younger bull who had been following the herd. The older bull was confident and answered the eerie squeal once or twice, sprayed his underbelly once or twice with urine, and resumed his grazing, not budging in response to the bulging duet that developed.

Two archery hunters moved through the spruce and pine forest, with its small openings, toward the nearest bull. When they were a half mile away one of the hunters took out his call. Hand heard the second call and knew it was minutely different from the first.

His phantom grew close as memories of D. James, Molly and the bugle call surfaced. Darting in and out amongst the ghosts were the longer, uglier shadows of the old bull squirming, smells of blood, man and the gleaming deadly instrument. He shook his mighty head; it was as though a great tidal wave was cascading over him. He returned the call with magnanimous force. The hunters knew that this squeal was from the trophy elk that everyone in the area wanted to bag. They realized also that to do it would take skill; that they would have to behave like a roaming Wapiti bull. They would have to imitate a feisty bull, one that wasn't afraid to move in to get the better of the harem-guarding bull.

Hand judged how they advanced on him and he was concerned to avoid a disadvantageous position on the steep hillside. He maneuvered to keep his hillside position. The hunters moved forward, timing the calls, and they also added the yelps of the urine-spraying behavior to indicate that the approaching bull was confident and ready for battle. Hand hadn't moved but he did respond again in a distinctly nasty fashion. Puzzled, Hand discerned that the challenging bull phantom was advancing on him because the second and third calls had sounded closer than the first. The seasoned elk turned, charging in the direction of the vibrating sound and adrenaline flowed throughout his large frame. He stopped and raked his antlers against a young spruce tree. The hunters responded by working over a similar tree with a big stick.

The hunter bugled at Hand again, and he answered. Then

the old bull horned again, and the hunters saw his dark antlers rise and fall, but not a hair of his body was visible. On he came, heading straight for the men, his body shielded by a pine tree twenty paces or so in front of them and his antlers protruding beyond the trees on both sides.

In a few seconds Hand had moved around the tree, snorting and prancing for the charge. It was too late to retreat. The hunter raised his bow in that split second that Hand left the shelter.

The bull's guts were on fire. Nothing could stop him. The phantom had materialized. He no longer charged another bull, but rather his target was the ghost, the creature of conflicting smells, sounds and experiences. The arrow found its mark - a perfect shot through the heart. Hand took two steps, still shaking his mighty head and emitting furious snorts as he took the third step on the now stick-like legs. He caught the strong comforting goat odor, and then he fell forward and toppled full length into the earth's giant arms, embracing and cuddling him as though Molly is near, and the warm liquid is oozing out and around his soft muzzle.

One of the hunters rushed over with flashing knife blade extended and neatly ended Hand's existence.

"What a kill, just look at that spread!" the bugle blowing hunter, Nat, said.

Al wiped off the knife before replacing it in the scabbard. "We're lucky, I tell you. The old fellow was mad, crazy mad. I never saw anything like it. If I would have missed, unlikely but possible, -- he would have kilt us both." He rubbed his ear and continued, "Never saw anything like it - a crazy bull."

Nat shook his head and bent over for a closer look.

"Say, what's this?" he said, reaching for the ear with the tag

"Why, I'll be darned. It's a cattle tag, but there aren't any number, on it, only GOAT."

Al moved in closer for a look. "GOAT. Now ain't that something. You know, I had to milk the nanny this morning as my wife went to visit her folks over to Appleton County. She likes the dang things around as pets; they're real nuisances. Hell, the old bitch almost kicked me out of the barn. Doesn't like me at all."

The two men stood looking intently at their crazy goat trophy bull.

"It sure is something, the GOAT on the tag, it sure is. We might as well get on with it. It will take some time and it's getting late."

"Yeah," Al agreed, removing his knife.

The blade caught the last gleam of the sun's light.

# Return My Soul to Me

Return my soul to me.
And you will surely see the
Change In me.

Please return my soul to me.
Too long you have wondered,
Too long in that sea of freedom
Without our melody.

A life of futility,
It was, tending to the ways
Of humanity.

Then my soul fled.
Fled my earthly ways and aims.
Fled from the fruitless happenings of
A life devoted to falsehoods given its way.

Please return my soul to me.
Listen to my plea.
A heart within is changed.
God has shown his love to me.
To one such as me
God has shown his love.

My aims are now a
Search for truths,
In Justice that they bring.

(January, 1976. This poem was written on a long winter evening in front
of the fireplace.)

# The Horse Trainer

"A horse is not a machine controlled by instincts. They think for themselves. Yes sireei, they can think for themselves," Kyle said as he walked with George Waller towards the horse trailer and pick-up.

"I'm sure you're right, Kyle. I've heard good things about your horse training. I wanted the best for Thorney. A horse with his personality, gentle yet full of energy, is rare. Did you notice his lines?"

"Yes, sir. I sure did. He's the closest thing to a perfect horse you'll ever see. I plan on going real slow with him."

"Fine, I'll call in a week or so to see how you're doing," George replied, shutting the pick-up door.

Kyle watched the tail end of the large horse trailer as it turned the narrow corner past the bridge. His eyes traveled quickly over the horse as George had led him out of the trailer. The black horse had moved with the grace of a gazelle. He was a 'mixture of quarter-horse and thoroughbred, and it seemed he had the best qualities of both.

His muscles rippled revealing his strength, yet his delicately shaped head was characteristic of the thoroughbred. His long legs appeared strong like the quarter horse, but his graceful movements reflected the high-strungness of the other. The neck was slightly arched, ever so slightly; the nostrils flared or seem to, and the black eyes: He had the blackest eyes Kyle had ever seen. These three qualities dazzled Kyle's imagination. "Here," he thought, "is a horse for the gods." He remembered studying mythology in high school and had envisioned Zeus, the god of lightning riding through the sky on a perfect horse, a black horse with stark black eyes.

Hurriedly he strode to the corral behind the barn for a long look at the perfect horse. The young animal was pacing, with his head arched and ears pointing forward, black eyes surveying his new surroundings. Yes, Kyle knew he had found the perfect horse. He had an uncanny imagination regarding animals, especially horses. Since he had decided to become a horse trainer, each horse he had trained so far had been special.

51

He felt that he could communicate with a horse through their body language. They were like people in that some wanted to please and some were independent and stand-offish. Others were timid, while others were stubborn. And they were always fearful of the first training. It was his job to quiet them, to get acquainted; and know that he cared, communicating to them his concern. But here, this was something different. This horse made his blood race, his heart beat; a horse for a god, a perfect horse, and he was the trainer.

Realizing that Thorney would have to be returned changed his mood. A horse like this should not have an owner, not like he was a pick-up, or a new saddle or tractor to be shown off. No. Not Thorney. He belonged to the gods.

Kyle shook his head to dislodge these fantastic thoughts. He was a dreamer, the target of his uncle Harry's ridicule. But he would go slow, very very slow with this jewel.

Thorney stared at Kyle with the haughty black eyes, suddenly snorted, and shifted his forelegs. Kyle was again fascinated. "What a horse," he thought, budging open the gate with his knees and walking towards the proud animal with small even steps. The young horse's head jerked higher, and with equally small steps he started to move backwards. Then Kyle's smooth voice halted his progression.

"Quiet, boy, quiet Thorney. I just want to get acquainted, just want to get acquainted." Kyle continued to take steady steps closer and closer to the horse who watched him so intently, all muscles taut ready to leap away if necessary, but whose ears pointed forward as though he, too, wanted familiarity. Kyle could now feel the taut energy and smell the sweet horse odor. Reaching out, he gently began to stroke him; the coat felt like velvet and Kyle's heart beat. Thorney was a perfect treasure, not a horse!

That night, Kyle's dreams were filled with images of the perfect treasure, the horse of the gods. He was astride the mighty beast, and what a horse it was: All fire, powerful as gunpowder, untiring, enduring, obedient to whatever Kyle put him to.

The dream changed as though by a magic switch, and Kyle found himself trying to coax a cat down from the top of an electric light pole. Then there appeared rows of poles with cats, all crying out in fear from their lofty perches. He was again astride Thorney, racing down the pole corridor, running to escape the loud shrill cat moans.

When he woke, his body drenched in sweat, memories surfaced recollections that he had pushed aside. It had been Uncle Harry who had shot Stormy off the pole. His great uncle Harry had always lived with them and had been in total charge following his father's fatal accident when Kyle was nine.

He remembered how the cat had been a perfect cat. It reminded him of Thorney—the same independence and energy intermingling with a gentle inquisitive nature. And such a beauty, deep orange with white stripes and bright green eyes. He had slept at the foot of Kyle's bed. He was never the master of this splendid animal – no one could be. This individuality is not, and could not be conquered. Stormy had simply been his companion and friend, that's all.

As he looked at Stormy's cozy spot on the bed, memories of one cold windy night flashed before him. The wind had beat furiously against the small but secure ranch house, and Stormy hadn't returned for the night. Stepping out the back door, he had called, screaming out against the wind, but there had been no response. He had slept restlessly and was up early to search. Huge snow-drifts attested to the strength of the abated storm. The quiet scene was disturbed by loud shrill meows coming from the direction of the woodshed, but he couldn't see Stormy. It was then that a small group of barn swallows had taken flight, and as Kyle watched their ascent, he saw Stormy perched on the pole. Standing knee deep in snow, he had urged, coaxed and pleaded with him to come down. The frightened cat had remained motion-less, emitting low pitiful cries.

His family was now up, his quiet mother going about the breakfast work, his father and uncle were grouchy as they had to get the caterpillar with the snow blade to open the road so his father could go to work at the saw mill in Elkton. It would do no good to ask his dad for help. So that left Uncle Harry who was in charge of the ranch chores. The back door slammed shut and Harry stepped out on his way to milk Hazel, the brown Jersey cow.

"Can't do nothin' for that fool cat. He won't come down and he'll freeze. You don't want that, do you boy? And you ain't finished your chores. Your mother's 'bout out of wood."

"Please, Uncle Harry, please," Kyle was crying. "Can't you call the light company? They'll get him down."

"Not today, they won't, not after the storm. The electricity is probably out in the valley; can't bother them today."

Kyle had lost control, cursing and screaming until the large man grabbed him by the collar end smacked him across the face.

"You're acting like a sissy. Come on, get out of here. I don't want another word out of you about that damn cat. They's a dime a dozen anyways."

His mother only nodded her head as Kyle repeated the story, her emotionless face not showing that she had h e a r d .  S he continued to stir the biscuits as though all was well with her world.

It was then that they had heard the shot. Kyle ran out the back door and saw Harry standing under the pole with the gun. The cat lay like an orange rag against the snow where fine traces of red spots gathered around the still figure as though to mark the scene forever.

Kyle tore at his uncle who pushed him away. The young boy crumpled over, pushing the snow against his face. He wanted to hurt, to feel physical pain to release the inner agony.

Kyle stood, not wanting to remember, and walked to the window for a glance at Thorney. He now knew Uncle Harry for what he was, a sad, awkward old man who had to be in charge. His manliness depended on it. Creatures like boys, women and animals, especially horses, were to be handled. Understanding did not help him to care for his uncle. He had been handled too many times. The uncle's authority had yelled out at his mother following his dad's death. "He'll soon be a man. Quit spoiling him. We don't' want no sissies around, now do we?"

His mother hadn't answered, only shook and lowered her head. It was as though she too was a scene that had been marked with blood, here own life's blood.

Kyle reached for his faded blue jeans, pushing away these negative thoughts. Nothing would go wrong—nothing. Why ole Uncle Harry could barely get around. All their farmland had been leased out to the O'Connor Brothers. Kyle worked for them, not for his uncle. He stepped out of the bedroom and rushed outside. He would have time to see Thorney before breakfast.

Stopping I half way along the path, he listened to the early Spring birds' shrill chirps. Hurrying along he reached the corral where Thorney was pacing gracefully, alert preparing for the day. Kyle entered talking softly, edging near with small steady steps. Thorney didn't run but glided backwards slowly. And with each step, Thorney's black eyes flashed letting Kyle know about his space - a space that emanated from his splendid individuality. It was not to be tampered with. Kyle instinctively knew this. He was not the master. They could only work together in mutual respect, and they were beginning to do so through this dance, this silent communication understood only be the horse and the young man.

Kyle had been so focused that he didn't hear Harry hollering that breakfast was ready. The old man then wandered down to observe.

"What's wrong, boy, you've gone crazy over that horse. Why don't you let me show you how it's done. Tie him down and jump on and let him buck til the devil's outa him. And if that don't work, I've got my ole horse club out in the oat bin."

This speech broke Kyle's concentration. Shivers overcame him as he yelled "I ain't never, never goin' to use that club. you hear?"

"You young fool, you just like my daddy's brother. He was a crazy animal lover too. Went around doctorin' all the horses and cows in the county. The folks there finally had him put in an insane asylum the day after he tried to take the wart off the only good eye belonging to old Jake O'Conner's cow. The cow went blind and had Siamese twins the very next day. Folks thought he caused it all. The twins are still in the museum there in Stonewall County stuffed and all stuck together at the neck and shoulders. Yup, they had only one large neck between them."

Old Harry laughed as though telling a good joke. But Kyle only shook his head. He had heard the story hundreds of times. Wearily he trudged toward the house, opened the back door, and entered the kitchen.

His mother stood beside the stove holding a cup of coffee. She looked up and placed the cup on the stove top and started to dish up his breakfast. He stared at the plate piled high with hash browns, eggs, bacon and biscuits.

"Why do you cook all this every morning? It's just me and Harry and he don't eat much these days. They won't be hired hands no more."

She stared at him with her black eyes, the only feature in her pale drawn face that seemed alive. The small narrow nose and thin line for a mouth resembled the careless strokes of an artist. But the eyes - the black penetrating eyes, - what sorrow and mystery hid behind these deep recesses? The thin mouth opened as though by another's command.

"Why, Kyle. You know your father always expected a big breakfast and his father and my father before him. What would I do if I couldn't cook for you and Harry? Why it's not even work any longer, just something I do."

It was not the answer that meant anything. The answer was routine. It was the eyes, the black eyes, that gave Kyle his answer, an answer he didn't want to hear.

He hurriedly ate as he was late for work and then darted out the door and ran for the old green pick-up. He wanted to drive fast--- very fast—away from memories of the dead cat, his mother's eye, his Uncle Harry's horse club. They all screamed at him like the wind on that night long ago.

The morning's sunlight peered gently through the side window caressing the left side of his face; this soft warmth mitigated his anxiety. Thoughts of his horse training pleasantly came to mind. He had ordered a complete set of books on the subject from *Western Magazine*. He had read and reread. It was great. The author was in tune with what he had always thought.

"Always keep attention between you and the horse. Face him, eye him and start sensing how the horse feels towards you. Never mount a horse until he is quiet. Don't push. Wait. Go slow, talk, as bad habits can be formed, habits that take hours of unlearning— so go slow." These tranquil thoughts were shaken as a far away echo of his uncle's voice pushed forth like a bully elbowing his way through a crowd.

"Go slow? Why go slow? I'll get my horse club out of the oat bin. Go slow, hell: I'll show him who's boss."

Kyle pushed hard on the pedal; the old pickup leaped, rattling and shaking, its old body wasn't accustomed to this new energy. Kyle didn't care; he only wanted to get away from the imaginary

56

elbows—pushing and shoving—always pushing and shoving. The warmth of the sun's healing rays calmed him as happy thoughts once more swam through him.

"The first time mounting, flap hat gently about the head. Do not overdo. Do not train a horse in a corral that is real small as this is fearful for the animal. It is important that it can feel space."

He pulled into the O'Conner's driveway past the old garage that had been converted into a machine shop. Odds and ends of old machinery parts lay scattered about the building. The two O'Conner brothers stood near' the rear of a large cattle truck engaged in an important conversation."

"Can't figure where we went wrong, Bennie," the younger brother said. "It sure looked good, real good when we started to expand."

"Sure, it did. But who knew the market'd suddenly drop? Politics, goddam politicians have their fingers in everything these days," Nat snapped angrily.

Kyle knew immediately it was the same talk from yesterday, and the day before, all the way back to the collapse of the wheat and cattle markets. They, like the rest of the ranchers, were so far in hock that the bankers could be foreclosing in the Fall. Times were bad, real bad, there was no denying it. His mother's black eyes now elbowed their way into his thoughts. He brushed his hand across his forehead as if to wipe away the hard-time eyes.

Nat liked to show off his friendly nature by slapping Kyle on the back and asking how he was doing. Kyle usually answered "fine," but not today.

"Great. I have a new horse to train, and he's beaut."

"Oh, now come on, Kyle, a horse is a horse, and if it can't work all day, it ain't worth its feed. A great horse is big and sturdy, but a beaut, no:" And Nat laughed.

The familiar suffocating feeling again overwhelmed him as Uncle Harry's harsh voice scraped him unmercifully. "Get the horse club out of the barn. We'll teach that 'beau' a lesson."

"Ah, C'mon, Nat. Leave the kid alone. He's gotta ride the south ridge and we got lots of work," Bennie said while glancing at the field beside the barn and shaking his head.

Kyle saddled a large dark sorrel horse with a thick ugly neck and chest. The early Spring day had now begun, the wind blew

57

cold off the nearby mountains. Kyle knew it would even be colder on the ridge.

"Damn," he thought, " I was in such an all-fired-up hurry to get away that I forgot my mackinaw. I'll freeze:" He then saw an old tattered denim jacket hanging on a peg behind the horse stall. He grabbed it and led the sorrel out of the barn.

The jacket was too large and was stiff with barnyard dirt. A horsey smell intermingled with a musty odor reminding Kyle of the mice and rats scurrying across the floor and hiding in the granary where Uncle Harry's horse club stood against two large grain sacks. The mice had eaten holes around the sides of the sack. The tiny grain seeds had attempted to escape only to be stopped outside the hole. Too many tiny grains had jammed together acting as a plug. The small seed mounts stared out like eyes.

Kyle opened the large wooden gate, and mounting King started for the ridge. The jacket's odor was unpleasant. In his mind's eye stood the horse club and the staring sacks. He urged King into a fast gallop to get away--far away. He then tore off the coat and flung it alongside. It fell and then crumpled as though dead upon the ground. Kyle watched its brief descent. It was like flinging off all the sneers, smirks and rude remarks. He much preferred to shiver from the cold.

Kyle sat on the fence watching Thorney. The long day at work was over. "What a magnificent creature," Kyle thought as he slid off the fence with halter in hand. Thorney and he again went through the same routine. It was like a square dance, moving forward and then back in rhythmic unison all the while reading each other. Thorney's black eyes flickered, ears moved forward and then back, head arched and tilted. It was the same even when the halter was secure against his alive and delicate head and face. Or does a horse really have a face? Not really, but the eyes, the black eyes seemed to be the face, the total face. Kyle wasn't really leading him. They were merely walking around the inside of the corral together—master and horse were one.

Kyle continued to go slow with Thorney, and all thoughts of the horse's eventual leaving were tossed aside. Several weeks passed before he mounted the perfect animal. Kyle had taken

Thorney into an open field, and even though it wasn't necessary, he had flopped his hat gently about the horse's head. Thorney shook his head as though ridding himself of a frisky horsefly, and the black eyes sparkled as he nudged Kyle with his head, perhaps telling him to quit all the foolishness. The saddle and bridle had gone on without trouble. Thorney merely twisted his head and neck around for a look. Kyle carefully put one foot in the left stirrup to let Thorney feel his weight, and then in the right. And Kyle was in the saddle. Thorney leaped forward and then started to twirl in a circle as though seeking his friend. Kyle spoke and rubbed his neck reassuring him "I'm right here, boy. Now we can take flight together. Easy now, boy, easy."

George was becoming impatient. When he called, Kyle always had reasons why Thorney should stay longer. One day Uncle Harry answered.

"How do I know how long that fool boy'll take? It seems he has to teach that dumb animal love before he's finished. If I could've used my horse club, you'd a'had a well-broke horse weeks ago."

"Well, I don't like the sound of that, but can you tell Kyle I'll be over Saturday for Thorney. If he ain't broke by now, there's not much hope," George answered abruptly.

Kyle was not ready for this news. Surely something would happen before Saturday. He had been riding Thorney every day and how they complimented each other. Kyle felt the graceful, gliding motion of the perfect horse. And he also felt his great spirit, something one didn't tell folks, especially Uncle Harry who would have called him a crazy horse lover. It tore at him like a knife through his guts. Thorney would be leaving: His precious jewel would be out of his life forever.

In the evenings, Harry poked at him constantly mentioning Thorney's departure and how the dumb brute could have been broke weeks ago with the horse club in the oat bin, the oat bin where the grain sacks had sprouted eyes.

By Wednesday evening, Kyle noticed that his mother's black eyes flared in anger at Harry's jibes. But she said not a word in Kyle's defense. And Harry continued on and on. "You're spoiling that horse, boy. I'm telling you for your own good. You're damn lucky George is getting him on Saturday." Kyle didn't answer but stared out the kitchen window getting a glimpse of Thorney

59

waiting by the gate. Thorney now waited morning and evening for his friend; it had become a ritual for them.

That night Kyle had another dream. It was a brilliant morning. The sunshine danced as he walked to the corral. The birds' song rang out greeting the sun's rays. Everything seemed alive, vital, and he was part of it; the trees, buildings, a living and penetrating universe. Thorney, waiting by the gate, was part of the cosmic dance. But when Kyle reached the gate, Thorney was gone, and his mother stood in his place staring out from the confinement with her cryptic black eyes. The sun's light disappeared, and in its place an ominous black shadow appeared. Kyle shouted in horror and terror, throwing his hands over his face, screaming "Mother, Mother! What have they done to you?" What's wrong?" His mother spoke as though in a trance. "They broke me in with the horse club, son. Didn't you know?"

Kyle woke sobbing, spasms penetrated so deep that he was almost senseless when morning arrived.

"I'm going over the mountain to look for work. One of my friends works on a ranch there. Maybe he'll help me. I have to get away," Kyle said not daring to look at his mother. "I won't be here Saturday. Just tell George I had to leave; something came up."

His mother stirred the biscuit dough indifferently, shaking her head in agreement as though all was well with her world.

Kyle couldn't watch her. Running upstairs he started throwing odds and ends of clothing into an old battered suitcase. Anything. It didn't make any difference. Nothing mattered, nothing at all. The dark shadow had settled upon him. He had to get away, far away.

Thorney waited the two mornings after Kyle's departure for their early morning ritual. When his friend didn't appear, he became taut and nervous, alert as though preparing for flight.

Saturday morning arrived. Thorney was at the gate waiting when his owner approached. He was confused. Where was Kyle? The energy in his muscles exploded, and like a cannonball he shot across the corral. Uncle Harry came down out of breath, eager to help. "The boy took off over the mountain. I'll help you. He's sure frisky this morning."

The two men walked towards Thorney hoping to corner him. The angry horse twisted out of the trap, racing to the gate whinnying for Kyle, his head held high and his black eyes flashing.

Uncle Harry's broad face seemed to spread when excited, and the nose overgrown like a squash vine wrapping itself around a corn stalk. His tiny beady eyes traveled all around. "You stay here. I'll go get my horse club out of the oat bin. I tried to tell ya that that boy didn't know nothing about breaking horses. Why did ya hire him for, anyways?"

George looked confused. "But I thought you said the horse was trained as Kyle has been riding him. Why's he acting so foolish?"

"Yeh, I did say that. But it appears that he ain't really broke. I'll saddle and ride him the right way."

"No, I don't think so. The club isn't necessary. Where did you say Kyle went off to?"

"He done run out on you, and it's plain to see why," Harry said. And not waiting for further arguments, he rudely turned toward the barn. He then stepped out of the building carrying the horse club in one hand while dragging the saddle and bridle along with the other.

Two pairs of black eyes followed Harry. The pair from the corral stared, muscles tensing, taut, ready to spring into action. Tears fell from the black eyes staring out the kitchen window, but, the mother continued to wash dishes, the worn hands sliding across each plate and then into the steaming hot rinse water, slowly, rhythmically as though all was well with her world. She didn't bother to brush away the wetness from her wrinkled cheeks, but let the salty water spread over and down into her brown and gold blouse. The tears belonged to someone else, not her. She had ceased to cry years back. Finishing the dishes, she turned a-way from the outside view. Her world extended only as far as the small fenced-in yard with the few flowers and shrubs. What went on "out there," beyond, was no concern of hers.

Thorney edged his way towards the far corner avoiding the men and their shadows. Closer and closer they came, defiling his independence. He reared, jerking and pushing his long graceful legs into the air—striking out—escaping the gloomy uncertainty. Where was the gentle voice that had calmed him?

"He's mad. What's that fool boy done to him?" George yelled. "Get back. He'll kick you."

"I'll get the lariat. We'll have to tie him to the post," Harry said, pointing to a large pole in the middle of the corral. "I've broke many a horse tied to that post." The old man looked like an excited fledgling flopping on the ground.

It didn't take long. Thorney was lassoed, and his head was yanked tight against the pole. All he could do was strike out with his hooves, and every time he did so, Harry whacked him across his rear flank with the ugly club. Harry believed that his method was quite humane as the rear end was his first target. And if the animal didn't behave, he went for the ribs, the neck and finally the head. Every attempt at saddling was met with a flashing kick. Thorney's spirit was strong. Harry's beady eyes jumped with anger. The face seemed to spread, and the nose clung as though choking life.

George was also excited. He tried at first to restrain Harry, but it was useless. Harry's fury only increased. Thorney was in turmoil, the horse club thudding against the ribs and then the neck, back and forth across the animal's beautiful flesh.

Thorney's loud eerie screams now filled the air. All the animals shook with fear. Betsy, standing near the corral, began to turn aimlessly in circles.

Kyle's mother was sorting the wash on the back-porch laundry room. Thorney's screams penetrated the very heart and soul of the house; even the fine particles of dust seemed to utter tortured cries. It was everywhere. There was no escape, except for the mother who refused to yield to the horror. She continued to sort clothes, darks in one pile and lighter colored in another, as though all was well with her world.

And then, as quickly as it had 'started, it was over. The house became silent like an Egyptian tomb. Harry had clubbed Thorney on the head and the blow had brought him to his knees. He was semi-unconscious. He could move, but it was with great effort as though he had suddenly been switched to slow motion. He staggered slowly to his feet, finally untied, swaying like a lone yellow willow tree touched by a gentle yet strong breeze. Harry placed the bridle bit between his teeth, pushing it up with one abrupt thrust. He then raised the saddle onto the swaying back. Thorney was in a trance, as though all was well with his world. Man, and beast then staggered slowly around the confinement. A silly grin spread and covered the human's face as though he had won a great battle. The owner suddenly came alive.

"Come on. Get off, goddam it. Can't you see he's sick?"

Harry yelled back. "Sick, hell. I just got the fight out of him, that's all. In a day or two, you'll be taking him on a pleasure ride."

"I'm not so sure. Now get off, Harry. I'm taking him home."

George didn't take Thorney on any pleasure rides. He couldn't ever get close to him. He called in an attempt to contact Kyle and Harry had answered.

"I'll be right over. He just needs another workout."

"No thanks," George yelled. "Just tell the boy I want to talk to him."

Harry wouldn't listen. With the club in hand he rushed over. It took a considerable amount of willpower and finesse for George to deter him.

No Harry. We've been friends and neighbors a long time. But you're not touching that horse again. And where the hell is Kyle?"

"Don't know and don't care. He's run off. No respect for nothin. I tried to tell his mother she was spoiling him," the old man replied as though apologizing. "How's about one more go round. I'll fix him, I know I can."

"No! Now get on home if that's all on your mind. The horse is ruined, can't you see?"

George telephoned again. Kyle's mother answered in an indifferent voice.

"Gone over the mountain for work. Don't know when he'll be back. He hasn't even sent his address."

George gave Thorney a week to rest, and then tried again to get near him. It was no use. The black eyes flashed as he reared away, striking out with the deadly hooves like the uncoiling strike of a rattlesnake. George called old Doc Edwards, the county veterinarian, to come over.

"Ain't much I can do for him, poor devil. Appears as though he has suffered some brain damage. I've seen it before. Some become so sedate and mild that a two-year-old baby could ride them, and others go plum loco. Someone used the horse club on him, ain't I right?" the old-time vet said, glaring at George. "I've seen many a good horse ruined. It's a pity, a real shame, but they won't listen."

63

George stared back and then lowered his head. It was plain that he wasn't going to answer.

"You might as well sell him for fox feed or to the glue factory. Put the poor creature out of his misery."

"Sure hate to. Just look. Such a beauty. Damn!"

"Well, I hate to see this. The glue factory would be better, but young Tom Sellings is starting a rodeo string up by South Bend. I vaccinated some of his new broncs yesterday, and by the looks of that horse, he'll make a hell've a bronc."

George sold Thorney to Tom. Dr. Edwards had to be summoned to tranquilize the horse to get him in the trailer. One hundred fifty dollars was the agreed upon sale price and Tom seemed pleased.

"This is the first time I've had to calm a horse. The devil is in that horse and look at those black eyes. Maybe I've got a famous bronc on my hands," he said, shaking George's hand. George turned and walked quickly away.

Kyle heard about Thorney's fate two months later. He had thrown himself into summer ranch work, working long hours in hopes of forgetting the perfect horse and the strange dream. Towards the end of August, he had to drive a truckload of hay to Elkton, so he stopped by home. He hadn't really wanted to as he didn't want to hear about Thorney. But Uncle Harry was there accusing him.

"What did ya do to him? And then ya run off and leave me to take the blame. George thinks it's all my fault. Why I oughta smack you, and I would, too, if you weren't so big. Harry's beady eyes flipped, and his face started to spread. Kyle's mother stared at these two men from the strange outer world, her face a plaster of Paris mask.

The same look was settling upon Kyle. He shut out Harry's accusations. He could only think about Thorney, the special, perfect horse that belonged to the gods. He was now lost forever, driven and showed around the tough rodeo circuit where the animals lost all their selves except when on display. Then the cowboys and fans would call out their program names, calling and swearing at them to buck even harder.

Shivers pulsated Kyle's body. Righteous rage mingled with sick impotence. For a moment he wanted to beat his uncle with

64

his own ole horse club from his butt to his sorry head, but the man was too easily broken and pathetic to deserve attention. Let him baste in his own wretched bile. He wanted to scream at the rodeo coliseum spectators that they were torturing the gods, that horses were not machines to be handled, but they would only be baffled while holding their beers. Some of them actually appreciated the hearts of horses who would not be broken.

Kyle's agitated spirit was overcome. He had had delirious sleep with tormented dreams since he heard about Thorney. He couldn't run far enough. He couldn't bury himself deep enough in work. He had a yawning revulsion at the thought of freezing his heart and face like his mother. But what? Shoot Thorney with dignity and end his tragic misery? Steal him in the night, and go where, pursued as a thief? Would Thorney still know him, recognize him, respond to him, or was he too senseless and traumatized?

A woozy image worked its way up through Kyle's nausea that brought a hazy clarity as it hooked his almost numbed curiosity. Escaping with Thorney in broad daylight with everyone witnessing it, and their knowing on some level what was at stake for boy and horse? A confusing, yet improbably hopeful image. He left without words to walk it through in the live silence of the outdoors.

The next rodeo was Sunday, and Anna headed for church, like she always did. Church was a peculiar space for her inbetween her restricted inner place, and that outer world of avoidance. It had a soothing ritual quality to it like washing the dishes or clothes. She steeled herself up to go every Sunday, not al--lowing Harry's comments about sissy Jesus-lovers making pointless trouble handle her. Part of ritual church was kneeling in a back pew by herself with her eyes down, not having to engage anything, with a priest sensitive enough to let her be. She had a puzzling relationship with this strange, suffering God who had been misunderstood, betrayed, beaten, and killed, but still claimed this unsure life. It tickled some deep part of her, but she couldn't yet translate it into her heart, voice, eyes, and face.

She also felt relief in confessing. She had not been able to bring herself to stand up for Kyle or herself, but she prayed that the wounded One would help somehow.

Anna remained kneeling following the services that she mostly blanked out, and when she left, all was quiet outside. The people were gone. Walking toward the pickup, she noticed that the tire on the left rear was flat and there wasn't a spare. She walked toward the rodeo grounds. Harry would be there and maybe Kyle. She purchased a ticket and then sat on the top row in the stands, away from dealing with anyone, but having a good view of what was happening.

Behind the bucking chutes, Kyle stood by the corral gate peering in at the broncs. Thorney stood alone, apart from the others a short distance from the gate. His ears were forward, head moving slightly as though trying to remember where he had heard the soft gentle voice. He lowered his head and moved slowly toward the comforting' sound. He now stood beside the gate, flashing black eyes staring at Kyle.

The young man returned the stare, still talking quietly, hoping to sooth and heal Thorney's torn psyche. The old familiar energy surrounded horse and man. Thorney trembled as recognition swept through him. Kyle's hand reached out caressing the head and neck that had been bruised and beaten. And with the other hand he opened the gate where the bridle had been thrown across the nails. Continuing the gentle touching, he slipped the bit between the downtrodden animal's teeth and then up over his ears. It was on. Kyle's muscles were taut now that escape was near. It was then that Harry walked towards the outhouse and saw them.

"Hey, what's going on? What are you doing with that horse?"

Thorney reared back, snorting and striking out at his enemy. It was time. Kyle quickly lowered Thorney's head with the reins, then flipping them over his neck, jumped on. Thorney felt the weight, reared and leaped forward racing past the startled cowboys. Harry ran after them shouting "Damn thief! Stop you young fool!" Tom and a group of cowboys joined in. But man, and horse were now racing around the track towards the opening on the far side past the grandstand where the woman sat perched on the very top.

A smile suddenly illuminated her face, cracking the plaster mask that had held her face tight into tiny chips and pieces. The black eyes flashed with excitement and surging with a new life and freedom, Anna screamed out joyously. "Run, Thorney! Get away, far away!" She clapped her hands and jumped up as all seemed well in her life.

"Leave me alone, Harry," Tom said. "I've heard enough about that horse from you ever since I got him."

"But shouldn't we go after him?"

"No. If that boy wants him that bad, he can have him. I'm sure he'll pay me the one hundred fifty."

Harry walked away angry and defeated, and as he walked past the grandstand, he heard Anna's startling happy voice call to him. "Harry! Harry: I'll need a ride home. The pick-up has a flat tire."

## Sunflowers

Sunflowers, oh so tall
Share with us the
Mysteries of immortality.

Sunflowers, oh so tall,
Growing there for all.
Each little seed bringing
Forth serenity.

A stalk bears its load,
Without a thought or misery.
Growing thus a tiny seed,
From last year's serenity.

How fast it grew into
A look of majesty,
Standing there for all to see.
How fast it fades and yet
Remains a fact
Of immortality.
A fact of life, so profound,
I have found without
A frown, from the sunflowers and
Their seeds.

A fact of life is the seed
That continues on
We can see.

A truth of immortality
We see, continues on in our posterity.
These realities of life
Are there for all to see.

Sunflowers, oh so tall,
Is the love of the all?
Somehow the mystery
Of immortality?

(This poem was written In January 1976 beside the fireplace. It was written for Lynn Ann with the thought that she could, perhaps sing it. The idea came to me after reading Plato's Dialogue, "The Apology" in which Socrates examines the question of immortality while he is awaiting execution in prison.)

# The Toilet Paper Thieves

An old lady draws open a pair of dirty, tattered cream-colored drapes, and peers out vacantly. There is nothing, or almost nothing, visible, unless the dense San Francisco fog is something.

Martha Kaufman is 96 years old and hates life with a yawning, cavernous, vengeful anger. She feels as though she has been betrayed by one of her lovers, or a husband, three in all (and how many lovers? Even she is uncertain). She hasn't any children, so she cannot blame them. No, it is Life, or rather the Old that is her enemy.

Old surely doesn't exist by itself in time, and as some thinkers would say, it doesn't exist at all. Or as the philosopher G.E. Moore says about "Good" being indefinable since it is simple, not having parts like the natural objects in the world. Good likewise doesn't exist by itself in time.

Old is also simple, not having parts, and is indefinable. But as far as Martha is concerned, so damn what! And not just Martha, but *everyone* knows that both Good and Old exist somewhere, somehow, sorta, like the dense San Francisco fog ethereally surrounding everyone and everything, and without having parts.

Well, the Old does, but maybe not the Good.

Martha had dashed, skipped and jumped over there and over here in her younger years. She had miraculously kept this eager vitality till she was 86 or thereabouts. She had enjoyed her lovers and husbands in that order. She also was involved with nature. She liked to classify and film everything in sight, or rather everything but rats, mice, flies and fleas, and those sorts of things. Flowers, plants, butterflies, deer and eagles, now *those* are the cream of nature's crop, not rats, mice and fleas.

She enjoyed her career as a CPA. She was a whiz, a genuine genius with figures. She had accumulated quite a large sum, difficult to know exactly, but there was at least $300,000 in her savings account, plus monthly dividends from stocks and bonds; all of this plus her monthly Social Security check. She had also taken up foreign languages at age 75 or 76 to aide in keeping her mind keen. She traveled, hiked, and probably did other things that were enjoyable.

So Old, that invisible foggy something or other, did not catch up with her until about 86. Old then ruthlessly ripped with its ironclad invisible hands, not releasing its hold, and Martha despised this foggy something or other, hated it passionately, because she could no longer escape from this inexorable enemy.

It appeared at a first glance that she had merely given herself over and her abode had turned into something resembling a tomb. But she only *appeared* defeated. She was *not!* She counted her money daily; pennies, large and small, and lived frugally, like a church mouse, although she didn't film rats and mice and such things. She had sustained herself with just her Social Security check. Pennies from the dividends joined the growing family in the bank.

She didn't use her money to get help for her apartment, shopping, and other tasks that were difficult, even impossible for her to perform. Consequently, the dirt, grease, grime and spider webs accumulated in her dwelling. Piles of dirt and dust, raggedly dirty drapes, dingy gray walls, were everywhere, until at last her habitat became the tomb, cold and death-like.

One day three years ago, she fell and broke her hip. Even then she refused to secure help. She crawled up and down the 84-step flight of stairs to her apartment. She had two walkers and left one up at the top of the stairs and the other at the bottom. The old woman eased out of one of the walkers, whatever the case may be, either up or down, and then crawled on her stomach and arms, sliding along like some old snake (she did film snakes in her younger years, but not rats, mice, flies, fleas and things like that). If she should be at the bottom of the stairs, she then pulled herself onto the first-floor walker and hobbled to the bus stop, and then on to the shopping mall.

What a sacrifice, what a woman! Surely, she is saving her money for some special cause, something grand and worthwhile; something that will expand life, not just the mere ability to exist. Even animals manage to exist. No, a grand and worthwhile cause that will lend itself to the process of fruitful living, where new insights are not brushed aside like the pesky gathering of dust on furniture, and other such things. And then Old can take a back seat. What is a tomb-like residence compared to such a sacrifice?

71

Evidently her grand plan does not include her grandniece, Annette. Annette has health problems resulting from an automobile accident, a serious illness involving years of struggle and hard work. She does not stop to plead with life. No, she forges instead into what she feels is the main task of living, which is to ask questions about existence. She refuses to be conquered by what some of the existential philosophers describe as facticity and fallenness. Facticity encapsulates the circumstances of an individual's life, family background, talents, personality, time in history, schooling and other influences, all the large and small *cringing gravities* of life. Added to the formidable list is what has been called Fate.

There are others who contend that luck and bad luck do not depend upon Fate, but rather the individual is responsible for his/her own fate. This awesome responsibility includes accidents, illness and even death. We control these misfortunes with our attitudes. Negative thinking promotes the Bad things, while positive attitudes bring about Good things. Now it is understandable why Martha didn't film rats, mice, flies, fleas and other such things.

The above is a very foggy argument, as foggy as the Old, Good and the Bad. Fallenness, as described by Heidegger, is the tendency of humans to cluster together and define existence through each other. This creates a certain cringing, obsequious mode, where people are not individuals in their own right, but are more like mice.

Annette doesn't care for this cringing, clinging set-up of Fallenness, but finds it difficult to locate her own promised land. She has studied and has obtained a doctorate in Philosophy. But she is out of employment and can't work at most jobs due to her chronic pain problems, except for a few part-time positions with low pay. She is looking for teaching positions, and these also will be difficult. She is a writer, bur writing is slow and tedious as the pain in her arms, neck and back surge through her, taking hold, gripping in, like the Old.

She decided to write a letter to her great aunt. She had considered doing this for the last five years, but never quite had the courage. For one thing, she didn't want to beg, and she felt Martha wouldn't understand the gravity and yet the splendor of her situation. Her aunt might even become angry. But Annette's circumstances had taken a sudden twist toward Bad Luck. (Is this Fate or is it caused by her own attitude?). She had to quit two positions due to the pain. She had just enough mortgage money for two months, very little for food, and no money for toilet paper and the other extras. Reluctantly she wrote her aunt to sign over her small house as collateral to sell, though it needed repairs large and small, and she had nothing with which to repair them.

And so, a business-like letter. Her house as collateral for a loan. She couldn't ask her son and family who were also living without enough money at the time. The fog was again appearing. Annette also asked her old aunt not to be angry, that it was merely a request, and she could purely and simply say, "No, thank you."

Martha received the request letter two days ago. Without a thought, without a nod, grinning to her self-made self, she had discarded it, tossing it aside like it were some old dirty shoe.

Now the old lady closes the drapes and decides to go out in spite of the extra dense fog, in spite of the Old and the Good. It is no longer necessary for her to crawl and roll down the stairs. Her hip has healed, but the trip is still difficult and slow, one step down, or up, and then another, one at a time. It is only her strong, relentless Will that moves the old body along.

T.S. Eliot once mentioned a stick-like body in one of his poems. It seems to go something like this: Man is but a paltry thing, a tattered shirt upon a stick. Martha's Will is being obstructed, as her Body rebels against the unreasonable tug-of-war. This Body is thin as ice, and is tired of being tugged, moved and shoved here and there, like some old gunnysack. It hates Martha's Will as much as Martha hates life. This Will is like a club, a deadly weapon, inexplicably demanding the frail Body to march on and on, and for what? This is the question, and there is no answer. It does seem, however, that the old woman clings to a life that she hates because she enjoys counting her pennies, large and small.

Today her Body, unaware of the fatal consequence, ended its battle with Martha's Will. *The Body wins*, right in the middle of a busy intersection. The Body stops and the Will loses as it can no longer budge the Body. The light changes and a motorist seeing only the green light and not seeing the body until too late, hits Martha's Body and Will. The Will isn't injured. It merely fades away, like the fog, but the Body flies through the fog, along with the Old, the Good, the Bad, and then it falls down on the pavement.

Martha dies the next day. She gains consciousness long enough to instruct the nurse to add her dividend check to her pennies, large and small, and for what?

Her niece Helda has been appointed executor for the estate. She arrives on the plane the next day. The ordeal of Martha's life confronts Helda with vigorous potency. The tomb is filled with junk and other things, but mostly junk, odds and ends, mementos, bits and pieces of life, clinging like rats to a sinking ship. After taking a taxi to the apartment Helda sits facing the dirt and grime, knowing she must stay. She hasn't money to go elsewhere.

Suddenly the phone interrupts the silence. Helda jumps at the unexpected intrusion. It is Martha's lawyer calling to give her instructions. Helda is bewildered, confused. She is not used to these transactions, not at all. She has lived on a farm in northeastern Oregon most of her life. She has cooked, cleaned, worked, and struggled in order to raise a large family, plus all the extra tasks and chores necessary for rural living. For forty some years she has labored without praise or support, and for what?

And now this big town lawyer is giving her instructions about how to sell Martha's stocks and bonds, regarding the funeral arrangements, the bills to be paid, the apartment to be cleaned and cleared. She must keep records of all her expenses and make an itemized list of all valuables for tax purposes.

"Cremated. Oh, yes, Mr. Helm, she definitely wanted to be cremated. She mentioned this only two weeks ago in a letter," Helda answers. And again, "Yes, yes, oh yes, of course I'll open the safe deposit box tomorrow." Again, she listens, "Yes, yes, oh yes, I found the keys in the top drawer of the desk." Pauses--"Yes, yes, I'll bring the contents to your office tomorrow. Yes, yes, thank you. Good-bye." Helda sighed with relief, replacing the receiver.

The appalling yeses still linger in the room. "I swear on all that's right I'll never say 'yes, yes' again. I'm sick of it all, obeying others, husband and children, and now a lawyer, and my mother. I used to jump when she called and demanded. I'm sick of it all - sick of the yeses, she convinces herself, and pounds her fists together as if the lawyer's head is in between.

74

She glances around and tells herself that first things must come first, which calls for an external cleanup. The internal one will have to wait. She must clean the bathroom and the kitchen, or at least remove the top layer. It is not an easy task to clean up after someone else, especially if that person hasn't cleaned for years. She rubs away the obvious layers of grime in the kitchen.

She stops in the door of the bathroom. Here, in this room, there is something spellbinding, shown in the possession that is an embodiment of Martha's past. She can see the busy years, up to age 86 or thereabout, when she had style, grace and fastidiousness. This something from the past is an ordinary household item, but people do not think about it, nor do they talk about it, nor do they give it as a wedding shower gift. Others would laugh and make fun of them. In Martha's bathroom, on the toilet paper holder, is a less than half a roll of light toilet paper with yellow and darker pink flowers swirling around, as though they have been perpetually uprooted.

Helda looks at it and frowns, remembering how five years ago, about the time when Martha had begun to hate life, and Helda had made her last visit, how she had gone in to use the bathroom, when she had heard Martha's strong, mannish voice yell, "Don't use the paper on the roll, use the other on the stand!" And on the stand had been a plain roll of white toilet paper.

Helda looks and, sure enough, there is another white roll. Helda now knows that Martha had stolen it from the hospital where she had done volunteer bookkeeping every Thursday. She knows because she saw rolls of it with MD printed on the side, piled in the closet when she had hung up her jacket.

She also notices that the pink roll looks the same as it did five years ago. "It's the same, I'm sure of it. She put it there to accent her decor." To prove it, she dampens the sponge and scrubs vigorously at a small area on the wallpaper. Before long a yellow color emerges along with some dainty pink and yellow-orange flowers. "Of course," Helda exclaims," the reason for the pink flowered toilet paper."

She looks at it in disgust, loathing the old roll of paper. She cannot touch it, she never will, not ever! She decides to leave it for the new tenants, leave it as a token, a sign of Martha's grip on life, a hold that has evaporated into the foggy non-future, and all

75

that is left of the fatal grip is the faded pink toilet paper; the extraordinary household item, not to be given as a wedding or shower gift because people would laugh.

After removing the top layer of dirt from the bathroom, Helda feels a "pinch of salt" better, that's all, just a bit better. The apartment still resembles a tomb, musty, rank smells penetrating the room. She shivers. She feels like Antigone sitting in her very own tomb awaiting her very own death. At least the kitchen and bathroom are cleaner, mediocre cleaner. This will have to suffice.

She sinks into the elegant rocking chair and begins to rock, a movement that has always been soothing for Helda. It is as though she associates this motion with something pleasant in her life. Perhaps it reminds her of the gentle rocking motion of love making, or the swing she loved as a child, or maybe both blending together. She didn't care to think. She especially did not want to think about Martha. Back and forth, so pleasant, so soothing to rock, like floating on a cloud where nothing can touch or disturb, a respite or a haven.

And so Helda quickly and easily falls under the spell of the swaying chair, a simple mechanism, primal in nature. But there exists another cloud. It is in the air. It surrounds her, not lethal, but dangerous to Helda's tranquility, dangerous enough that if it didn't poison her, it would at least leave her with the feeling of a certain imperceptible constitutional predisposition.

This other shadowy cloud was Martha's presence, lingering there as though on tippy toes, laughing at the set-up, a set-up of her very own making, giving her a strange sense of immortality. Her penny counting, large and small, had been a power set-up. The counting had imperceptibly created what she had desired. Subtly, cleverly, she had let it be known that she had money and she might, maybe, no promises, will some or all of it to this niece, that nephew, this priest, this cause, that friend. This then had been her great sacrifice, the reason for her frugal existence. She had counted her pennies, large and small, in order *to have revenge on Life*, one, two, three, and on and on.

Helda's rocking cannot escape the silent laughter, nor Martha's satisfaction in willing most of her pennies to the church for the homeless, people that she actually cared little about, or rather, did not care about at all. No, she had done it out of the spite stemming from her hatred of Life. She knew that, since she hadn't specified or hadn't wanted to help the homeless actually secure jobs or homes, that the money would be gobbled up in order to feed some of these people for a day or two. Or the organization would gobble it up in their great distribution systems.

This is sorta like when a mob hangs a person, and no one is guilty because everyone is guilty. The money and the guilt disappear into the fog, along with the Old, the Bad, the suffering. And *Martha had hated the Old;* nothing would be left. Nothing, just like the Old, the pennies, large and small would disappear *into the fog.*

Helda had received only a little more than the other relatives, Helda, she who had written and visited her aunt over the years, and who was sincere, simply because she was that by nature. Helda and her husband had given all their belongings away to their sons. These sons had had grand plans and equally grand egos and had speculated on becoming big-time ranchers. This seemed practical since only large operations survive; the small holdings gobbled up by the great. But the sons liked to count their pennies, large and small, and consequently had over-speculated and had lost the land to the Federal Land Bank.

Their Dad and Mom were allowed to live in the ranch house, their home of forty years, with most of the land lying idle around them. Their income is a small pension, so Helda did not receive enough to regain their lost land. She had had a dream. She had wanted to use the land to benefit others, but the counting of pennies, large and small, had consumed her dreams. Her small inheritance would be used in supplementing their meager income.

And so, it seems that Martha's laughter roars throughout the tomb because all of her money would be used up; used up, or merely added to the savings accounts of the other relatives for future security. And all would be for nothing, exactly like the end of her life, all for nothing. She had achieved her revenge. Martha's hatred retained existence, still lingering as she had created the nothingness; more of the same, her counting of pennies, large and small, had not been in vain.

Helda could no longer escape the cloud of non-thought, remembering another event that occurred on her last visit with Martha. Helda had taken the bus for two days and nights, and upon her arrival Martha had not been pleasant. The old woman had already started her penny counting crusade and had immediately informed her travel-weary niece that, in order to save money, they would eat out at McDonald's, and this would only be for a couple of lunches.

The first night they had eaten at home. When it came time for dessert Martha offered to give Helda a dish of ice cream. Helda refused it. "Why not, don't you like this brand?" Martha had hotly inquired.

"No, no, that's not it, one brand is as good as another. Anyway, I guess so. I just don't want any."

"Oh, all right then," the old lady answered angrily, flipping her head.

The following evening, they again ate at home. Martha was saving McDonald's for a big event. And again, Martha had asked Helda if she cared for ice cream. Helda reluctantly agreed, only to avoid conflict. But Martha was not to be placated. She waited until Helda was about to place a medium size spoonful of the ice cream into her mouth when she said, "You really shouldn't be eating ice cream as fat as you are."

Now Helda was not one to carry on. She had had a difficult life without much comfort or support from her husband. She had learned how to take the blows of life without flinching. But this time she acted out of character as she pretended to cry. She had gone into the living room, holding her hands over her face, sobbing and shaking, as though in great distress. Martha had been thoroughly shocked with this unusual behavior and had followed after her.

"Now, Helda, now calm yourself, there's no need to cry, no need at all. I'm sometimes too honest. Now you can't really blame a person for being honest, now can you?" she had said with her self-important self.

Helda pretended to stop crying and both sat awhile in silence, and then like a hammer crashing down on Helda's sincere head, Martha said, "You're too sensitive about things, Helda, you get upset too easily. I feel you need to see a psychologist."

Helda stared fixedly straight at Martha, the silence awkwardly consuming them like the fog, the Old and the Good. Martha, glancing downward, left the room. Helda remained, thinking that there should be a death penalty for verbal harassment that curled, curdled, and forever hurt and pinned the other; not caring if these others are sometimes children, young and vulnerable, destroying their emotional well-being. Forever pinning a child, like a butterfly, a badge; such deprivation, such desecration brought Helda to the limit of her endurance.

Helda shook her head, as though to dislodge these thoughts. It was not her nature to think like this, especially about the death penalty, revenge and such things. Her nature was for the most part, loving, and sincere. She mostly saw the Good, not the Bad, but not now, as a large amount, like a huge dung pile of verbal abuse appeared as out of nowhere and surrounded her like the fog.

There seemed to be box cars filled with all the nasty, mean things people have said to her, and to the people she loved; box cars that followed the engine placidly down the railroad tracks, not knowing and not caring where they go or what they do. "Yes," she thought, "the prisons would be filled with people awaiting ex-ecution, so jammed and crowded with verbal attackers that the system wouldn't be able to execute them fast enough to take up the slack."

Suddenly, without warning, Helda had a very disturbing thought. It was so clear that it resembled a vision. Helda saw Martha seated in the electric chair, all fastened in with ugly black straps, waiting for the deadly current. Helda realized that she was perhaps on the other side, and that by now she was secretly capable of doing unto others the things she had suffered. And Martha, sitting in the death chair, stared ahead from an ashen face while she looked younger. How strange for her to look younger, a woman of 96 to look younger before such a gruesome death, sentenced to die for her nasty, sharp tongue. And Helda, with an afterthought, adds, "She is also toilet paper thief."

The image vanishes and Helda walks to the window and, peering out, she sees the fog swirling gaily around and through the street lights, appearing as a lost halo. "What an unsettling image," she thought, "especially disconcerting because Martha had looked younger. Why is this?"

Not finding any answers, she ceased her rolling thoughts. And besides, Martha certainly had her pleasant side. There was a certain originality, a hidden talent, in the nature of her enemy and friend. She had enjoyed nature, the animals, and plants and could speak about these things with intuition and insight. And she never filmed rats, mice, flies, fleas, and other such things. She was witty, an excellent conversationalist. She had a certain grace and style about her, and she seemed genuinely fond of Helda, sharing the highlights of her life with her through their extended correspondence. And so Helda was fond of her aunt and hadn't wanted to continue with her troubling thoughts.

But the image of the execution had continued to haunt her. The younger face reminded her of someone she felt she should know. It had been Martha, no doubt about it, sitting in the death chair, but, paradoxically, there had been a younger person also, someone Helda should know, but try as she might she couldn't fathom who it might be. So tonight, five years later, as she rocks in the old chair, the image flares relentlessly. And again, there is the double face, the Young and the Old.

Helda's daughter, Sheila, arrives the next day with her pickup to help her mother load the valuables, dispose of the junk, and clean the apartment before turning the keys, after years, over to the landlord; not the same landlord, as the first two had died, one by the Old and the other by some disease or another.

The only items worth taking were a kitchenette set, the end table, and two filthy carpets. These were securely packed and arranged onto the pickup bed. In an off-hand afterthought, Helda placed the many rolls of toilet paper, with MD printed in large letters on their sides, into grocery sacks and then put them under the rocking chair and end table. The pink roll is left as a token to be used, or, more than likely, thrown into the trash by the new tenants.

The women attend the funeral. Martha had been friends with a French woman and her family for many years. The woman's daughter, Irene, had been especially fond of Martha, and had enthusiastically described to Helda the old woman's unique style and grace, her originality, her wit, charm, love of nature, her great intuition and insight. Helda had listened, believing and not believing. Had her aunt been a saint, a sinner, or worse, neither; merely an average person creating postures and images for others? For some, this image seemed to border on sainthood.

80

Irene did not mention Martha's nasty tongue, her counting of pennies, large and small, because these things were hidden from Irene. She saw only the favorable characteristics, and held true to these, reflecting her own self, as in "ain't she sweet?" because "ain't I sweet?"

Helda felt like a heel, like she was a culprit spinning the unsaid sinful vision; a sinner of sorts, and she couldn't even bring herself to think understandingly.

Irene graciously continues to praise Martha during the funeral. She ascends the podium as the priest is descending and shares a story with the five people, sitting like marble statues on the wooden church pews, directly in front of the podium. The group consists of our two women, Irene's mother, father and brother. The urn with Martha's ashes sits on a rather nice-looking wooden stand next to the podium, with the priest sitting in an equally nice-looking chair behind the podium and urn, and in front of the mourners. It is a rather nice-looking group, small, but nice. In fact, if one were to enter the large cathedral and see the small group, huddling like bats in a barn after a storm, one might think, "Oh, how nice," and not even know why.

Irene tells her story looking directly at the double doors, 'way, far away in the back of the church, as though waiting for a special critic. It seems Martha, quite before she had firmly began to hate to socialize, had attended a dinner with a man sitting to her right who complimented her by saying, "You're graceful, clever and interesting." The man repeated it three times, and eventually said, "Can't you hear me?" Martha had finally replied: "Oh, yes, I heard you. I just wanted to hear it again."

The mother, father, and brother chuckled, but not Helda. She felt like telling the story about the ice cream. She still couldn't "think understandingly." "Bet they wouldn't laugh then," she thought, and felt like a heel, a bona fide sinner.

The priest sprinkled the Holy water over the urn, using the sign of the cross, but the water droplets fell at random, destroying the sign. And so, the ceremony ended.

Helda and Sheila drive out of the city with their pickup load of so-called valuables, leaving the San Francisco fog behind. They stop in Ashland, Oregon, in order to visit Annette. Helda has been worried about Annette for years; poor health combined with a

81

strenuous life doesn't mingle too favorably. Annette was the daughter who had written the request letter, the letter Martha had tossed aside as though it were trash.

Annette was struggling with poverty and pain, and Helda couldn't help. She had given all her pennies, large and small, away to her sons, and they had counted their pennies and had invested the pennies until all was lost. They drive up and park next to a small apartment building. After getting out Helda reaches in the back of the pickup and grabs a sack of the stolen toilet paper. The two women ascend the two flights of stairs and knock on the door of apartment number 122.

Annette opens the door, her smile and hugs conveying her warm welcome. Helda quickly places the sack of toilet paper down next to a plant. The apartment has been freshly cleaned, hanging plants swing from the ceiling, others are scattered throughout the room. An imaginary warm breeze seems to be gently sweeping throughout the apartment, carrying the Good; a faint smell of lilac. The Old doesn't seem to be present.

The breeze blows past the almost empty cupboards and refrigerator, without questioning the whys and whats of the situation. The temperature of the room is below the comfort level. Again, the breeze doesn't question, but swirls around the plants and the freshness of Annette's home.

Helda disappears into the bathroom. She is surprised because on the roll is a half roll of pink toilet paper, reminding her of the roll left in the tomb. Annette's voice abruptly shatters her thoughts. "Please, Mom, don't use the paper on the roll, use the paper on the stand." Helda looks on the stand and there are two very small lumpy rolls of white toilet paper, without the cardboard holders. She glances up and observes that the bathroom colors are deep huckleberry and light pink, and she understands why the pink roll is to be left alone. It adds a touch of something extra-special, like a colorful personality flare, a blush at the right moment, or a smile and a wink at another, all adding spice to an ordinary life.

Helda re-enters the living room and directs a question to Annette although she already knows the answer. "Why isn't the white paper on the ordinary rolls?"

Annette answers and begins to laugh, her face ablaze with alive loveliness. "I have been stealing it from public rest rooms, a little from this one, and some more from that one, here and a little there, not much. And I save the bathroom decor." She stops because she cannot speak through her laughter. She finally resumes her dialogue. "Mom, I noticed the sack full of MD toilet paper. Now I'll no longer have to be a toilet paper thief. Was Aunt Martha one too?"

"Yes, I'm afraid so," Helda replies, not seeing the humor. Annette laughs louder and, speaking in an erratic fashion, in between the gales of laughter, she continues: "And I actually asked her for a loan. Two toilet paper thieves in our family, not horse thieves like in the old days. Good thing-- we would have been hanged. It must be in our genes, and Fate should have it that I get her stolen toilet paper." Laughter gaily rings around Annette.

But Helda is not laughing. She can't laugh because with Annette's words "we would have been hanged" the image appears, the two faces, the one Young, the other Old, but she now recognizes the younger face. Annette! It belonged to Annette, the toilet paper thief, and to Martha, the other toilet paper thief--but why Annette? She didn't have a sharp, nasty tongue. No, Annette did not; not at all. Why then Annette? Why? Why? Why?

Tears run down her face, tears that touch her soul in a way no other tears have or will ever touch her again, because the focus of the image, the two faces, Young and Old, Life and Death, reach into the abyss of existence, her existence, everyone's existence. It was Annette because of the counting of the pennies, large and small, and for nothing. They had won, the People Who Count their Pennies, Large and Small. And Annette has to sit along with Martha, waiting for the noxious current. The unquestioning breeze soars gaily upwards and downwards, without a discern able care.

## The Yellow Butter Cups

Tiny, yellow buttercups were there, I saw
Right there, on that early spring day.
A first sign of its coming.

Pushing their way up
Through the brown,
Cold, grass of winter.

Appearing as a smile on
A worn, sad face of sorrow, erasing the
Tears on the forlorn
Earth of approaching spring.

Even amongst the stones,
Forming somehow their solid mass
Upon this earth, I saw a tiny, yellow, buttercup
Smile between those rocks, and
Felt the sorrow of ages bygone and ages yet to come,
And yes, a tiny, yellow, buttercup
Was there on the face of each sorrow.

It is enough to make one
Hesitate and meditate a bit
Of the magnificence of a
Tiny, yellow, buttercup.

(April 14,1975. Darren and I had a very special day while taking a walk in the early spring. It had been a long, difficult cold winter and it seemed to me that Spring would never arrive. But, lo and behold, we saw the tiny, yellow buttercups and then knew that Spring would soon be there. I was so thrilled that I later wrote this poem.)

# One Single Thread

James absentmindedly kicked a small stone with his toe while keeping an eye out for the Bennet building. He was already late for his first Religious Studies class, which put him in an ugly mood. He wasn't keen on the class, but it was a required class as he needed 6 hrs of Humanities before graduating with a degree in Physics.

Spring was in the air. "Thank goodness," he thought, "I'll soon be out in the world with a good chance of landing that research job at the University of Chicago."

James spotted the Bennet building and looking again at his enrollment form, saw it was room 210 where the class would be held. Although his watch told him he was fifteen minutes late, he wasn't too worried, knowing he could slide quietly towards the back row without being noticed. No such luck. As James crept in slowly, Professor Mary Jane Ottoman saw him immediately, and halting her lecture in mid air, asked him to come up to her desk.

"What is your name and are you on my enrollment list?" she asked without further ado, penetrating eyes staring at him. James felt uncomfortable and switched his feet back and forth as though getting ready to run.

"I am James Newman, and I am on your list, or will be soon since. I registered late."

Mary Jane referred to her student list and seeing that his name was not on it, she promptly entered it. She was also aware of the precarious fact that there were now only eight students enrolled in her class.

Professor Ottoman was disappointed as she felt James, as a Physics major, would not be interested in a religion class. The subject wasn't easy to teach, especially if most of the class took it for requirements or electives.

"Now where was I," she said, looking out and over the heads of the students. Mary Jane didn't expect an answer. This had become routine over the years, trying to catch late comers before they changed their minds about the class. The Humanities has taken a terrible beating with the mighty scientific methods asserting only objectively measured facts were true while religious beliefs were mere myths or metaphors about reality, and thus secondary abstractions from the concrete, real world. Mary Jane, for one, was fighting against these blows.

Clearing her throat, she spoke where she left off about one single thread connecting all religion, and how we can, if we are serious and alert, have insights into these interrelated truths; how it is like finding gold at the heart of all religions.

It was here that Jodi Churchill, sitting in the front row, raised her hand. Surprised with the interruption, professor Ottoman nodded for Jodi to speak. Jodi was a serious thinker, always ready with questions. Her long blond hair spread out around her small features in what seemed to be an attempt to broaden her face. She had the peculiar mannerism of waving her upheld hand around in circles, even after being acknowledged by the teacher.

Jodi slowly lowered her hand, and sounding as if she were using a microphone, spoke with a loud clear tone addressing everyone in the room, including James who had already begun to tune out this religious "mumbo jumbo."

"If a single thread runs through all religions, why is there so much disagreement, and why does God seem so far removed from the world?  It might be a single thread of some sort, but it simply doesn't reach far enough." Upon finishing her thought, Jodi's tone of voice grew softer, and her arm and hand fell limp onto the table.

Mary Jane answered through honoring Jodi's concern. "Yes, this is a problem and I hope that now the class has been alerted to what I define as a 'Core Problematic.'  There are no unquestionable answers, but we can seriously investigate, study, and use the dialectic process to come to some sort of agreement concerning human realities that seem to ring true on various levels. While we cannot define or describe love without remainder in a test tube, we can have helpful encounters and reflections about it that help us gain access and perspectives in relation to its undeniable power."

Dr. Ottoman's lecture continued without further interruptions. At the end of the class she pointed to the blackboard and read out loud a short take home assignment:  Prepare a short paragraph describing your first remembered image of God.  Then compare and contrast these memories with your current image of God.

James reluctantly copied the announcement, thinking it was a silly thing to do. He walked past Mary Jane, giving her a nod on the way out. Although James, with his huge hands and feet, felt awkward at times, he now made quick work with his stride to catch Jodi who was just up ahead. As she turned and smiled, flipping her hair away from her cute face, James managed to clear his throat and ask her what she thought of the assignment.

Jodi gave him a generous smile and replied, "I don't know until I have time to think it over more, but it sounds interesting. I suppose that all we know about God are through images, myths, and metaphors we have encountered along the way."

A growing sense of disinterest took over as James let out a dreaded sigh, "I guess so . . . well, so long. This is where I turn off. See ya next class!" The thought of seeing Jodi's beautiful smile again gave him the much-needed incentive to get to class tomorrow. With that final thought, James made a right turn heading for his car.

Mary Jane allowed the students time to get settled with note papers and pens resting neatly on desktops. She began with a short lecture about talk of God. "Talk of God revolves like a wheel turning, while the hub of the wheel remains still. The stillness represents the hidden mystery of God, or the unknown God. Our language cannot penetrate this non dual stillness. Language is dualistic in nature, creating opposites, such as life/death, good/ evil, light/darkness, being/non being. We create forms or myths followed by metaphors, symbols, and images in order to express the elusive truth, the stillness beyond language. All talk of God conforms to these forms and are in their nature anthropomorphic, which is defined as using human char-acteristics, such as love, beauty, goodness and all-knowing and all-present as the creator God, and many more in hopes of moving closer to the center of the stillness that is indescribable."

Mary Jane turned briefly towards the blackboard, and then facing the front she asked who would like to present their assignment first. In spite of the many willing hands that shot up, a surprised James Newman bolted straight up in his seat as he unbelievably heard Mary Jane call out his name. Eyes darting to the left and right, large feet prepped for escape, James felt his face flush and chest pound with terror, dumbfounded as he had pushed the silly assignment from his thoughts, thinking he could coast through the lecture unaccounted for. Again, he heard it, "James Newman." Why did the sound of his very own name bring a sudden sickness to his gut? "James? Would you please share with the class your own response to yesterday's assignment?" So much for slipping through the cracks.

He heard an adolescent; cracking response emanate from his mouth. "I, uh, well, I uh . . . hoped to . . . could I (clearing his throat) . . . need to be excused...?"

Professor Ottoman knowingly smiled as she gently responded, "James, I can certainly understand your apprehension with the assignment, yet it is of the utmost importance that you take this class and the given assignments seriously as I believe you will find yourself surprised at the end of this term. Please feel free to open your heart and mind and genuinely search your soul as you soak in your fellow classmates' experiences. Really dig down deep, James, and we'll all be anticipating what you find as you share with us tomorrow."

At that, James quickly mumbled a thank you as he slunk low into his seat, pen in hand ready to take notes.

Professor Ottoman then turned to Jennifer Hayes sitting in the front row. Jennifer was an older than average student with short brown hair and eyes. She had experienced many difficult events in her life. Inner wounds were beginning to heal, but time was needed for further inner peace. She spoke in a precise manner, as though giving order to invisible entities. "When I was five or six, I thought of God as some kind of huge spirit-man that could be everywhere at once. I didn't understand how this could be, but my grandmother said that was the case and I should believe it."

"I then saw a picture in the Bible where he looked rather like my grandfather. This was Jesus, and I was told he was both God and man at the same time. I carried conflicting images around within me until I reached thirteen years of age. I then dismissed it all until a couple of years ago."

"It was an ordinary happening that changed me. I was attending an AA meeting. I was voicing my testimony, 'My name is Jennifer Hayes and I am an alcoholic.' I was just beginning to tell my story when in walked a very short monk. He was wearing a long brown habit and walked with a slight limp, dragging his left foot along as though it didn't belong. The door was left open, and the wind was whipping at everyone. The brown robe flew up and back revealing a faded pair of old tattered jeans. The monk kept walking right up the aisle, not a least bit concerned that his main bit of clothing was now swirling around the back of his head. Then I had a thought that appeared out of nowhere. 'Under the surface, the monk looks as normal as any other guy. But monks are representatives of God, and so God must be just as normal and approachable as any other guy.'"

"This image or insight penetrated into the depth of my being, held there for further transformations. The monk sat down near the front row, and as I continued my story, I noticed he was smiling with splendid heavenly hilarity. The door was now open for me to fully realize that God was close at hand in the most ordinary sort of way. "

Professor Ottoman was pleased as this response encapsulated the reality of both an imminent and transcendent God. She spoke briefly about this connection, hoping to plant the seed for further discussion later.

She then called on Brad to share his images. Brad was a small man in his late twenties, with large teeth and rather small eyes that darted here and there as though trying to catch something in one large gulp. He felt unprepared, but speaking in a loud voice, hoping to ease his nervousness, he began. "My first image of God, I think, emerged with belief in Santa Claus or Ole St. Nick. Santa with all his magic reminded me of God who I heard could do the impossible, and Santa was a loving fellow giving toys to all good boys and girls. God favored the good also, even to the extent that there was a hell where all the bad people went. I then decided I liked Santa best."

"I left these childish images behind years ago. I have since read many spiritual books. One book I really like was *Seek the Source*. I have travelled many thought-miles in my quest for Spirit. I have obtained many images or concepts about God that give my life meaning. I fully realize, however, that concepts must become realizations before I can truly understand or have inner transformation. So, I wait with full attention for God to be revealed."

Mary Jane made a few comments again concerning anthropomorphism and images of God. Then Jan Elliot was asked to present her response. She was tall and slender and sat sideways with her legs crossed and partially in the aisle. She seemed to walk, sit and stand with an overflow of confidence. She swallowed and cleared her throat a couple of times before beginning. "When I was six or seven, I thought God was like a judge who sat on a huge throne where he gave out rewards to some and punishments to others. I never thought that he actually loved me. I tried to imagine a judge-like person as loving me, but I couldn't. Although I did listen when the minister spoke about God as love, I just couldn't bring it home to me."

"As I grew older, the precarious judge was toppled by a grand image of God, or so I thought. I read about concentration meditation in my study of Hinduism. I decided to try it in my own simple way. I would sit very still concentrating upon an object. Any object would suffice. This required patience and a sense of letting go, of stilling the mind to not be centered upon one's self. After many attempts, something happened one day. I had been concentrating on a beautiful flower vase. It was almost a light shade of blue, except it was more like a delicate grayish green with a burst of light yellow and a sparkling light red. These colors were swirling around as though there was no separation, all seeming to be one. I felt very peaceful and actually in love with what seemed to be another level of reality. The experience lasted only for a few minutes, but it has given me new meaning and a genuine hope for greater transformation and understanding. Also, I have since been more loving towards others. My thinking is more open and less judgmental, and I feel an expanding energy of sorts."

Mary Jane quickly mentioned that Hinduism was to be studied later in the class, and that this response paralleled the famous Hindu saying, "that thou aren't." Mary Jane defined another term, "Mysticism," and noted that Jan's response represented the mystical path. "I am not talking about pseudo mysticism. I want to emphasize here and throughout the class that mystical experiences are unique individual experiences."

Kristi was asked to share next. She was a large lady in her early thirties, struggling with life due to circumstances beyond her control. She worked hard in an attempt to overcome these obstacles. She stood up slowly and faced the seven faces in front of her. Hesitantly, she began, "I was raised by atheists, and the only God image I had was also the judge sitting on the sky throne judging others. My parents informed me that there was not a God at all, and especially not sitting on a sky throne."

"So, my image became a non-image, a mirage or a fantasy. I like animals and one day I saw on TV some psychics who could communicate with dogs and other animals. This got me to thinking about God or the 'non-god' of my childhood. If some people have the talent to converse with animals, it seems reasonable to ascertain the possibility that both humans and animals have souls of some sort. If this is the case, then an entity more powerful than humans and animals must have created these souls. And if some humans who are superior to dogs can communicate with them, then the powerful 'Creator of Souls' entity could occasionally communicate with humans. I realize that this is a strange argument, but it seems to work for me."

"So, have I created an image of God? I really don't know, except to say, I no longer believe in my parents' non-god image. My image has a face of sorts and consequently has more depth. Or, am I now more serious, and I no longer remain in a closed system of a non-god?"

Mary Jane startle, fully awake. What a strange response, she thought. Speaking out loud, she said, "This is a very unique response, and I feel that it does inform us that God indeed is close at hand, giving insights to each individual accordingly. I feel Kristi that a seed has been planted in you that will mature as your consciousness continues to expand."

She called on Liz Warren next. Liz was twenty-two and filled with wonder and awe over the most mundane things. She had a loud shrill voice that was annoying until one got used to it. Staring straight ahead, she took a deep breath, and letting it out, she glanced down at her response and started to read. "I was a slow child. I didn't walk until almost two and didn't talk until almost three. I have been told that I was a watcher; following, observing, staring at everything that surrounded me. As I watched and listened, I understood God to be someone very important since he was everywhere at the same time. Also, God was either angry or happy with me based upon my behavior and thoughts. My parents who I thought as being very big and powerful, were lower than God. The God word stuck in my head, it was as though my image of God was the word 'God,' which was higher than anything."

"I stepped out from this concept in late grade school and high school. I became an agnostic. God is now a great puzzlement to me. I feel like a trapeze artist walking the highest wire. I have attended many different churches, and I have even taken Christ as my Savior, but I no longer feel the wonder and awe like when I was a child. I then read a passage from the Bible that said, 'Unless you become like little children, you cannot enter the kingdom of heaven.' I suppose that this is now my image of God. To return to my childhood, delight in things, but as an adult. So I guess that one must both take Christ as one's Savior, while at the same time become like little children before one can be saved. T.S. Elliot said this immediacy of childhood is the return to the rose garden. "

Mary Jane's energy was soaring with many thoughts and ideas from the responses. She felt it was going to be a great class where everyone, including herself, would gain new insights.

Jesse was next. He was thin and tall with a beautiful smile that emanated a great warmth, as though he was filled with sunshine. He spoke with a fast tongue, requiring the class to listen closely in order to understand what was being said. "My early memories of God were attending church with my parents every Sunday and also frequently during the week. I was told a great many things that I did not understand. However, there was one little reality that stuck somewhere in my little mind. This was that the minster spoke of Jesus as the 'light of the world,' and since I could not actually see Jesus or God, I wanted some confirmation of their existence. So, during service I would look at the candles sparkling with light and love and pretend that it was the light of Jesus and God."

"Also, I didn't understand how God was Jesus and Jesus was God. As I approached adulthood, I became increasingly aware of other things God was. These aspects were all clouded together in my mind. Like, he created the world, controls our destinies, resides in heaven, loves us when he's not punishing us, intervenes to performs miracles, sent his only son to die on the cross for us to save us from sin, and promises heaven for the devout.  He was a personal God and not the slightly chilly and unapproachable divinity one finds in the works of the protestant theologian Carl Voth. I was told a great many other things like the virgin birth, redemption, resurrection and incarnation."

"I became quite tired learning all these things about God.  I really didn't know how to handle it all.  I then came up with a wonderful image as I imagined that I put all things into a special place or enclosure called 'God stuff and Faith' in my mind or soul.  I had been told to believe these things with Faith or just because the Bible tells me so.  Now it was easy for me.  I could merely open my mind and tune into 'God stuff/Faith.'  This station encompassed all the good stuff in my brain. "

"There was, however, a problem concerning the Old Testament stories.  I will only give one example, since the one or two paragraphs assigned to this class has become excessive.  Many of the stories are very violent like when God commanded the Jews to annihilate Canaanites, which included all of the women and children.  I tried to put this new information about God into my mind enclosure, 'God stuff/ Faith,' but somehow it just didn't work. I was now perched like a great eagle of truth between the wonderful God of love and the terrifying God of the Old Testament. These two conflicting images were coupled with the words God spoke to Moses. When asked, 'Who art thou?' God responded with, 'I am that I am.'  These paradoxical images gave me a rational excuse to become an agnostic.  Just put it all on the back burner and let it simmer so to speak."

"I stayed with this program until my late twenties when I viewed a movie about the life of the Buddha.  I was thrilled with what I felt was a very strange religion.  And the more I read the more I was impressed."

Jesse was the last one to respond.  He waited patiently for Mary Jane's comments. "I attended church with my parents and my image of God was just that; 'going to church.'  It was something we did every Sunday and since God seemed to be the main attraction, I tried to imagine what he looked like. I closed my eyes and looked inside to see if I could see God.  At times I closed my eyes really tight.  I could then see flickering light emerge amongst the various shadows.  I then imagined the light was the forming of a figure that was perhaps a part of what God was. I then opened my eyes and took in a painting of God holding a lamb with other sheep close by. I liked this image a lot, and since I was told that Jesus was somehow God, I grabbed onto this image of God as a shepherd."

"I now feel that my image of God is intertwined with the positive side of ego growth. Potentials within each of us must be utilized to some degree for healthy ego growth to occur. Self knowledge can then emerge within the process of a knowing that transcends egocentric tendencies that is the negative side of the ego. Self transcendence appears when self knowledge enters the transpersonal realm of knowing and being, as it is precisely this affinity that connects being itself."

"The ego in order to remain in the realm of knowing and being must be included and then transcended. It is the turning of one's whole being towards a worldcentric realization. If the ego is left in the realm of egocentric realization, narcissism coupled with self interest results. A lack of real transcendence or value either with-in or without occurs. My image of God, believe it or not, reflects my search as a child as I am still stretching and straining to see God through the shadows of the egocentric self and the light of the worldcentric self. Being and knowing are joined as authentic self transcendence expands and incorporates a deeper reality not seen but heard throughout the self in relation to the outer. I realize that this response is too abstract."

James again stepped quickly out after class in order to catch Jodi. He spoke as they leisurely walked along. "I was not the least bit interested in this class or this assignment. I also felt that your question concerning the thin thread extending throughout all religions made total sense to me. But something happened to change my mind. I am still trying to assimilate or sort out these new insights so I can write about them before Monday. I'm glad that this is only Friday. "

Jodi listened with full attention and replied from the openness of her heart. "My experience or my God image was filled with mystery wonder and awe. It was both personal and impersonal--a real paradox."

"Yes, I recognize this, especially the part about the mystery. Say, would you like to have coffee at the beanery tomorrow

sometime? We can then discuss this whole thing more thoroughly. I have to hurry to another class," James said, with a smile that
would encourage anyone.

"How about two o'clock," Jodi replied, with an equally warm
smile.

"Great! See you then!" And with that, James spun on his
heel towards his physics class with an eager smile and a lighter
step.

Monday arrived and James walked slowly to class. His inner
self had not had time to assimilate the new knowledge or insights
forming within him. He still doubted what was happening to him.
Reaching the classroom, he smiled at Jodi and took a seat next to
her.

"Are you ready to tell your story?" she inquired.

"I'm still confused, but I will sort through some of my
thoughts."

Professor Ottoman entered the room and spoke about the responses, and how insightful they were. And then glancing over at
James, asked him to proceed.

James nodded, hoping to convey a much-needed patience or
understanding with what he was about to say. "I was raised
without religion, so my image of God was simply what I picked up
here and there in society. For me this was like another fairytale
like Cinderella, Pinocchio, Hansel and Gretel, etc. I am studying
to become a physicist and attached myself to the New Atheism
that encapsulates a deep belief in scientific rationality and
progress. My heroes were Richard Dawkins, Christopher Hitchen,
and Daniel Dennett. Daniel and Richard wrote the popular book
*The God Delusion*. All three support the New Atheism belief."

"Upon studying, reflecting and struggling with their theory, I
began to think about closed systems. In a closed system all
evidence against the system is rejected. The norms are created
that are no longer capable of pointing beyond themselves to a
bridge that can connect or glimpse the fleeting insights or moments that are essentially ungraspable in words or rational linear
logic."

"I also saw that every path to truth must grapple with issues of
the limits of knowledge, which includes scientific theories. What I
began to ponder was the intolerable intolerant certainty in the New

Atheism. It was always noon in Dawkins world, and the sun of science and liberal positivism was shining brightly, casting no shadows. I realized I was stuck in a form of Absolute Atheism, disallowing the ungraspable mysterious truths as a whole to penetrate my being."

"The thin thread that connects all religions also connects with the entire world. It was this thinking that affected my atheistic form of thought. To my surprise, I was no longer caught in the blinding totalizing web of a closed system. I must admit I now feel a strange sense of relief upon releasing this limited belief system, which definitely is a belief system, no matter its scientific trimmings. But the formless reality that I now confront will eventually form another Form, a Form that will hopefully be open and expanding toward a truth where the thin thread is manifestly present. The thread is a metaphor that can add and enrich, that can with any luck encourage an experience of ultimate reality at new unknown depths. It could provide a new language that becomes a harbinger to a fresh consciousness, challenging our assumptions and stretching us towards a new openness."

"Yes, I am now eager to learn about all the world religions and explore how the thin thread swirls in and out moving toward the fruitful reunion of both inner and outer realities."

Professor Ottoman, slightly taken aback by James insightful response, thanked James for a job well done. She began to speak. "Discovering the inner self is learning to give compliments to the self. It is learning to exercise this inner image and to continue to nourish it to wholeness, as the thin thread indeed connects the inner relation to the outer."

"We have time for comments before I start the lecture. I'll now turn the class over to James who can act as the moderator."

Jennifer quickly spoke up after briefly holding up her hand. "I feel that our thinking is beginning to ignore the mundane or real world for mere abstract concepts. James I would like you to talk about your two terms of formlessness in a more concrete manner."

Everyone thought this was a good idea; everyone except James, who was struggling, trying to organize and find the proper words to convey his newfound insights. In spite of his discomfort, he tried to answer the best he could. "I recognize that as an atheist or materialist I was caught in a closed system, essentially a lie, as I ended up dismissing all arguments against my theory, or more accurately, my belief."

"Some serious thinking and deliberation turned my closed system into a Form, or as in physics, a Pattern that weaved into and out of consciousness, organizing both how I perceived and how I responded. But in hard sciences, mind or consciousness is seen as a biological artifact, an accident of evolution, not as an order or complex pattern that requires something fundamental and unwavering in the universe in addition to matter and energy. However, I sadly felt that I was caught in a Pattern or a Form with my firm adherence to atheism."

"I desired to punch a hole in this pattern of thought that had such a firm grasp on my whole being. This was especially true since I would be learning about all the religions in this class that represent something substantially and universally human. As I described in my talk, the more open formlessness for me came when a hole was punched in the closed system. The Form disallowed possibilities or new knowledge to pass through my consciousness."

"I feel now that I am in a formless pattern of sorts that represents something fundamental besides energy and matter in the universe. The formlessness is actually nothing more than my ideas and beliefs changing, coupled with a letting go of the old to be receptive to the new that always was. A paradox emerges for me, but it seems that I feel to take in the new that always was can be seen as the old and the new being one and the same. The old way of thinking and being can metaphorically represent the form of thinking in a closed system, and yet the old is always connected to the new--it always was."

Jodi was at the coffee shop waiting for James. She was glad for the meeting, as she had been confronted with a problem concerning her career and was hoping he would have a few suggestions. She really liked some of his ideas, especially about form and formlessness. And besides, she was becoming quite fond of him

James was also eager to see Jodi again. He hurried to the coffee house, leaving behind some tedious lab work. He sat down beside her, and taking her hand in greeting, held it as though they were already an item.

Jodi didn't mind, as this simple caring gesture made her feel warm and good. For a minute or two, they were silent, each sensing that their friendship would continue to blossom. Finally, Jodi asked if he wanted coffee.

"Yes," he replied, thinking that was exactly what he wanted. And then, to just sit back, relax, listen and look at Jodi. She was a very lovely person, serious, and yet had a great sense of humor. It wasn't very long before James admiration required a more attentive stance as their conversation took on a more serious tone.

"I have been planning a career in social work, thinking I would make a difference. Then an event happened that has more or less changed my mind. My father died of lung cancer two months ago. It was a very sad affair," she said with misty eyes.

James squeezed her hand in sympathy as Jodi continued. "He was in a foster care home close by and either my mom, older sister or I spent time there giving him what comfort we could. At the end he was awake only at very short intervals and was on strong pain medication."

"For whatever reasons, there were various health care workers present. Some were nurses who were surely needed. Others were health care workers from hospice, while others seemed to be pretty floaty social workers from I don't know where! All of these workers gathered around the dining room table, scattering their computers and other electronic devices all over it. When my father Joe was able to briefly sit up, they would ask him questions that made me quite anxious about his well being. It also made me angry."

"One question was, 'do you know you are dying?'"

My father, staring out at nothing, nodded his tired head as though being interrogated by some strange entity who had been hitting him over the head with something other than a pillow."

"There were other insensitive questions such as, 'How do you feel about dying?'"

"Joe just ignored her altogether, and then said he wanted to go back to bed. "

98

"One worker sat at the head of the table and always had a large fancy array of instruments. She documented all of his information. I assumed it was all about how well prepared the patient was for his death, as if this were her main job, in addition to entering computer notes for insurance purposes."

"Another worker, sitting at the side of the table, asked how depressed he was on a scale of 1 to 10."

"Without blinking an eye, he said, 'Ten!'"

"She smiled sweetly and said, 'I will bring some antidepressants for you tomorrow,' and then continued to record on her computer."

James, listening intently as Jodi spoke, replied with concern in his voice; "It seems there are no good answers to a question such as 'how do you feel about dying?' For example, 'Great! I can't wait!' is a problem. 'It feels like shit,' not a good answer either. Asking how one feels about it is pointless without an appropriate response. There is a need for their jobs, but you can't train a person to be spontaneously empathetic."

"Exactly! It's so great to be able to express my feelings and open up and be understood! James, these people were heartless! What I saw and experienced through my father's death were trained, calculating machines, instead of warm caring, open hearted compassionate people. I'm worried that if I pursue this degree, I will lose my sense of compassion, and will be nothing more than a mechanical note taker. I care, I truly care. I want to make a difference. I'm so glad you understand."

"Yes," said James. "You do care, which is one of the things I really like about you. But it is like these helpers you encountered have some concept of what it means to be a social worker, but the rules and regulations of hospitals and HMOs have made it into a Form that actually limits their ability to live into the actual ideal."

"That's right!" exclaimed Jodi. "They present themselves as caring social workers conceptually, but they are not living it."

"Yah, your right," mused James. "There is a difference between actually embodying an experience and having a theory about the experience. Whatever concept or Form they are working with, is not helping them move into the experiential truth of the ideal. That's probably because they have an inappropriately scientific, mechanistic view of humans and what they need to live or die. That view certainly works better for computers. They need a more mysterious formlessness if they are going to deal with humans, themselves as well as their patients, who are not machines, but non-linear complex systems with non-rational hearts and messy minds of their own."

"Hey, well said Science Guy," responded Jodi. "So, if I know this, do you think I could go to Social Work School and come out the other end without being formed by the Form? a mere concept of a helper cut off from the ideal that motivates me?"

James thought twice before he spoke. "You know, educational systems and professional organizations who hold the relevant licenses really do exert a powerful forming influence on people. Look at me and the hold the New Atheism had on me. But heart hopefully wins out. You know, with the help of that Spirit-single thread thing, all the religions have a way of expressing. If anyone could, I'm thinking it is not improbable that you're the one."

And with that, along with a flip of her hair, Jodi took James' hand in her own and pulled him up excitedly saying, "Come on, Einstein! Let's go have some improbable fun!" The scientific, rational, James with his newly formless imagination, did not mind this suggestion one bit, not one nano particle bit at all.

# Branches Lay Stripped

Branches lay stripped
A melody within
Quietly waiting for a song to begin.
Birds of joy, birds of sorrow,
Patiently, meekly, seeking their song
Hovering high, descending low,
Wondering, puzzling where has it gone?

Flying, turning, running from the nest.
Crying, sobbing where is the song?

Oh, foolish birds of the air,
The branches must leaf
For the song to appear.
Gifted ones of God, a structure
Built without life will wither and die.
Songs will disappear.

Spring lies sleeping never
Dreaming of its song.
Never, ever, knowing, until
Grasping its hands of the
Limbs that burst into joy.
Then the song begins.

Creatures of joy, build your
Nests high facing the sun,
Sheltered from rain and floods.
The melody is there, a song must be sung.

(This poem was written in April 1972. It is my very first poem. I am not a poet, but for some reason when I lived on Indian Creek, caring for my four children, I wrote poems about how I felt and thought, as so much was happening to me at that time. This poem depicts the thought that what we must have is a life issuing forth from genuine caring and love before posterity and justice can authentically progress without inner conflict projecting violence and hostility. The birds symbolize children, reaching, yearning for this song of a real life. The idea for this poem took place early one morning as I walked along the creek in order to check cattle as the new baby calves were being born. There were many low hanging thorn brushes that I had to circle around and peer in to see if any cows were calving, hiding in the brushes.

It was then that I saw two birds circling and then sitting on the nest that was exposed against the bare branches. It was as though they were, indeed, building their nest before spring was there, and so the poem.)

# UP or IS IT DOWN?

I like bein' outdoors, even then at times, I want ta be indoors. This is how I talk mostly. I never seem to say anythin'. or almost never do I say anythin'. I'm used to it. I think I make sense. 'Cause it makes sense to me way down deep inside of myself. I, at times. trouble other people. They're apt to say I'm stupid or a bother. This is 'cause other people mostly ain't like me. They seem to have lots to say, very important things, any way I guess so, but I can't tell fer sure 'cause I don't understand them mostly. but I don't think they're stupid.

My ma, who works hard all day washin`, cookin' an' breakin' up fights 'tween me and my brothers an' sisters, she don't say much either an` neither does my pa, who works outside all day. My brothers, three of 'em, an' all of them older than me, an' my three sisters, all younger than me, don't say much either. So, guess we're jest that way, it's bred in us or somethin' like that.

I like bein' sandwiched in the middle, sorta like a piece of bacon, in them bacon sandwiches Ma throws together when she's too busy to cook a big meal. It makes Pa mad. He cusses an' says, "I ain't married ya t' be lazy." Then Ma cooks up a batch of her sweet rolls to show my Pa that she ain't lazy. It makes my mouth water jest to think about them rolls, hot ones, with piles of butter rolling down the sides.

Yep! I like it, bein' sandwiched in the middle, mostly 'cause no one bothers me much. I can go about invisible like, 'til one of my big brothers feels mean. like Pa is more times than not. I then gits picked on. I hate it and feel so low that I take it all out on my sisters. It's real fun sometimes to hear them scream and cry.

But Ma don't like it none, an' she stands me up straight, like a hitchin' post an' shakes me so hard that I can feel my head roll around inside. Then she grabs on to each one of my ears, all the same time, an' gives them a jerk. My ears are longer than they were last year an' if Ma don't stop this punishment. I's goin' to look like a dumb ol' jackass 'fore long. Ma don't pull my older brothers ears anymore and their ears still look the same as before. She don't pull them 'cause they are fourteen, sixteen an' seventeen an' bigger an' stronger then Ma.

Today is Saturday an' Ma fixed us some bacon sandwiches an` Pa tol' her she was lazy. We all are s'pose to put on our Sunday best clothes, and then go over to Luke Geigers old place, a piece down the road` or is it up the road, really can't tell fer sure. I s'pose it was Luke's place^ but not no longer, fer he is dead, guess it now belongs to Irma Geiger. Luke died on Friday after eatin' one of Irma's big meals, seems as if she ain't lazy like Ma. Ma Geiger, as everbody calls her, thought he was only havin' gas trouble in the belly, as he had real bad pain an' was lettin' out all the gas, stinkin' up the house. Irma nagged him an' complained so 'til she finally told him to git on out on the back porch, at least 'til he could quiet his belly down some. Ol Luke minded her fer about the first time in his life an' went out there like he was some ol` dog. He then fell over dead in his boots or in his tracks, as I heared my brothers an' Pa tell after killin' something. They love ta tell killin' stories, 'specially how the pore creatures fall over twistin' an' all tied up like they want to jump out of their skins an' git clean away from death, but 'stead they jest fall over in their tracks. Guess Luke's heart give out on him.

Ma Geiger felt real bad. I knows 'cause I over-heared - Tillie, Ma's friend, tell Ma about it. I was hidin' under the eatin` a left-over roll, piled up high with butter jest like I like them. Tillie told Ma that Ma Geiger was feeling real poorly, 'cause she shoved Luke out of the house-like as if he was some ol' dog. Tillie told that Ma Geiger says over and over, "I wouldn't even order a dyin' dog out like that". She then covers her head in her huge hands an' cries an' shakes all over as if someone was a torturin' her.

Tillie said she didn't know why Ma Geiger was so upset seein' as Luke hadn't been any fit specimen of a husband and had treated Ma like a dog more times than not. Tillie told Ma that only last Sunday she over-heared, by chance, Luke a-tellin' Ma Geiger to git into the carriage, jest 'cause she had been talkin' with Mr. Crow, the new school teacher.

Luke didn't like school teachers done, said they're better than ordinary folk.

My ma then spotted me under the table right before the good part about when Luke beat Irma 'cause she forgets to fit some ol' broken down somethin' sounded like a mostly gossip story, but Ma seen me before they finished tellin , and begun to speak at me in that unnatch'ral like voice again. It's like she turned from my ma who is sweet and nice, into a cross nanny goat and a half cawing crow or a squawkin'hen.

"Git on out from under that table, Bennie." She cawed and looked like ol' nanny getting ready to butt. "Yer jest like some ol' dog layin' 'round, lazy. Yer lazy, that's what. Yer goin' to turn out jest like yer Uncle Henry.

Chrise sakes, the old nanny, how I hate her when she's like that. She's not my ma then, no sirree. She was my sweet ma, til she talks like that. Tellin' me I might turn out like Great Uncle Henry. He was hung a whiles back for theiving. My daddy went down to the hangin' or was it up' can't really tell. He took some bacon sandwiches along. 'cause I seen him put them in his pack. He came home and says, "good riddance to him," like Uncle Henry was nothin' but a pile of trash or somethin." I poked in the pack an' seen that the sandwiches was gone. It makes me sick to think Pa ate them at the hanqin'. I don't like my daddy mostly, he's like Tillie and Ma said 'bout Luke bein' mean and bossin' everone around. It gits mighty, yes, god awful almightv confusin' tryin' to sort out everthin' down here or is it up here in this world.

Anyways, we put on our Sunday best an' went to Luke's wake. I don't like wakes, 'cause seenin' dead people is creepy an' makes me itch all over. Ever'time I been to a wake or a buryin' I git to itchin' somethin' furious. I told my ma an' even showed her the little red bumps that break out like chicken pox all over me. But she says she never heared of anybodv bein' allergic to dead people an' that I was jest allergic to somethin' else or was jest imaginin'. She said in her unnatch'ral voice, that I had ta go that 'cause a body had to pay their respect to the dead an' if we don't we

105

won't be gittin' no help, not an inch of help when we die. I sure don't savor the idea of dyin`, bein' stone dead, like them bodies I've seen. No, sirree, I can wait fer that. It don`t seem fair, first we're alive, doin' all sorts of things an' then we can, jest like that, be dead, an' doin' nothin' at all, but layin' in a box for people to gawk at ya. Can't tell if it's up or down--to die I mean.

We all crowd, like a bunch of hens gittin' ready to roost, all on one pole, into the buckboard. I got seated sandwiched between Bucky, my oldest brother and Sally Ann, my baby sister. I don't mind 'cause I can sit close to Bucky to keep warm an' Sally Ann clumb into my lap. I feel good aholdin' her. Babies are nice, even if they do cry an' make a bother, any hows they don't change into an ol' nanny goat an' a cawin' crow. They jest act like babies. Now with big 'uns, it's a story with a different color alt'gether. A body never can tell if it's up or down with grown-ups, or which side is up--the good side--or the bad side. Guess ol' Luke Geiger was mostly bad, anyways, that's what I heared while under the table. Now he's dead and I will soon be itchin' as soon as I see him. Ain't worth it, jest so I can get help when I die, no it jest ain't worth it, 'cause I don't need help from any big 'uns, babies maybe, but they're too little to help much.

I looked at the trees as we bumps along and begun to feel some better. I like trees, the way they all seem to respect on a'nother an' no one tree to better the other an' they are jest *trees, not up and* down, like grown-up folks are mostly. But guess they can't do nothin' else, bein' rooted fast to the ground an' all, can't do much else but stand around and mind their own business. Guess, they're sorta dead, not dead like Luke is dead, cause the trees were never a life like as Luke was a life. Luke was a life. bein' mean mostly. Trees do grow, bit by bit. Pa showed me the rings inside a big ol' pine he cut down and Pa said each ring were fer a year of growin' and we counted to see how old the pine was, it was lots older than Luke. A tree ain't good like a baby's good, 'cause a baby grows into a grownup and changes to the good and mostly bad, like

Luke and Pa. A tree is both up and down--up in the air and down in the ground.

I feeled all bumpy inside when we came to Luke's place. The road was bumpy, jest like I feel bumpy and uneven way deep inside gittin' ready to itch. The itch feels like somethin' real bad is tryin' to git under my skin, tryin' to crawl right under thar and grab me an' pull me down into somethin' I knows I won't like. Wish I was home hidin' under the table, eatin' a roll piled up high with butter. The itchin` is so bad an' it feels like I'll be pulled down to rot. that what the somethin' is I won`t like, rot, jest like a body rots.

Ma shoved an' herded us like a bunch of sheep into the house. Pa dragged along in the rear, not carin' to take part 'til Ma yelled at him, in her unnatch'ral like voice, fer him to git on along an' be proper. Like we enjoyed lookin' at bodies and hangin' 'round eatin' an' carryin' on like as if the dead was dancin' some ol' jig. Luke was dead alright, he ain't to be dancin` nowheres. I ain't old, only twelve an' a little bit more, so I ain't been around long enough to see a lot of dead people, not like I was seventeen, like Bucky. No, I've seen, now let me think, er--mavbe, nine or ten all told. But ol' Luke, here, he was the deadest person I ever seen. Can't tell why, but I knowed when I seen his face, all a gray color, like low hangin' smoke after a big fire somewheres. He smelled somthin' furious, nobody acted like they could smell anythin', but I knowed thev

was a-foolin' as to not upset Ma Geiger. Yep, I knowed as soon as I seen him. that even God Almighty can't raise him up anvwheres, or that the divil can't pull him down any-wheres. I knowed this, an` like I says, my family, it's inbred in us, not to talk much but ways down deep inside I jest knows some things. So, I won't be a-tellin' nobody. they won't listen an' say I don't make no sense anyhow.

I no longer thought to keep what I knows to myself, when I see the first bump come up on my arm close to my hand. It was a big `un, like a strawberry, an' as red as one. Then this itchin' begun. I never itched so bad before, I was makin' people stare at me. Ma don't like it none as she wants us to be proper. She changed into the ol' nanny right thar at the wake an' tells me to git on out to the buckboard. "An` you set out there alone, maybe you'll git some sense in you. Itchin' 'round like some ol' dog with fleas." Ma talked on in her unnatch'ral like voice, an' I hated the ol' nanny crow. ^A body ain't s'posed to disturb the dead, like that. Ain't I told you, you won't git no help when you die. Now stay." She told me this, "now stay" like I was some ol` mangy dog.

I sit thar scratchin` like someone gone wild. I felt like the bad was a-goin' ta git right under my skin and eat me. I could no longer sit thar. I had to git down an' run away from this thing, this itchin' that was gittin' at me, trying to git under my skin and pull me down into somethin` I knows I won't like. I ranned 'round an' 'round the yard ' til I was all played out an' jerkin' to git in the air when I jest fell down on the ground alongside the back porch. It feeled good to lay thar all tuckered out, not carin' 'bout the itch or nothin'.

Then I hears the back porch door slam shut. I looked up an' seen Ma Geiger standin' in the middle of the porch. Then I knowed she was standin' on the spot where Luke had died. I seen her face an' felt cold way down deep inside, cause she looked like somebody who had seen some terrible thing. Her eyes stared out into the awful nothin'ness, an' her mouth was pulled tight, making her face look all screwed up like.

Her face recollected me of the time I went with Bucky on his trap line. We seen a big wolverine caught fast in the trap. Right b'fore Bucky shot him the poor scared critter seemed to know somewheres deep inside that he was soon to be gone, fer a split second the snarl across his mouth left. He jest stood there starin' into the great nothin'ness. He faced me an` Bucky with his face all screwed up tight like as he was gettin' ready fer it. I got sick jest watchin', but Bucky, he seemed real proud of shootin' an` telled Pa all 'bout

I then heared Ma Geiger say, not very loud, jest loud fer me to hear. "He sure enough is dead, never seen nobody look so dead. Now why be that, do you s'pose? Maybe it's `cause he gone and

108

caught being real dead out here on the porch. I is responsible. I shoved him out. First time I order him out in ma life and he goes dead!?" She threwed her hands up across her face an` whispered so low I had to move myself closer to hear. "Why I wouldn't even do that to a dog, not a dog nor not nobody. "

"But what . . .. what if Tillie be right? Ain't it true he treat me like a dog all them years? No doubt 'bout that. But scriptures say treatin' someone as bad as they's treatin' you aint right either. But being a better wife to 'im then he deserved didn't fix 'im neither. Maybe like what the preacher was sayin about Jesus, riskin that 'is love could be lost on folks." Ma Geiger sighed, and I could barely hear her say, "So is carin' for an ole fool dog who don' get it, that thing called 'grace,' or is it just throwin' your pearls before hogs, 'er dogs? . . . . I wish ah' knew better which way was up."

## Among the Trees of Winter

Among the trees of winter,
I snapped a twig and then
Another.

The smell of spring was in the air.
Upon a branch a bird uttered its song.

Such sweet music echoed forth,
It held both soul and body in tranquility.

Upon my lips a faint smile appeared.
Soothingly it held me there.

The limbs grasped within my hands,
I held upright, marching proudly home,
Knowing that I held life there, hidden in the
Bare forlorn branches.
I placed them in water,
A miracle it was.

The life was awakened and
Beautiful green leaves appeared.
And this I did before spring was here.
And in my house the leaves emerged.

I look and see in wonderment
And know, that my spring also
Will be.

(March 1974. Again, it had been a tedious and long cold winter.
There had been days when I wondered how I could continue. This poem
brings hope of a Spring and fresh energy that seemed to appear in the
smallest of ways keeping me from losing the thought of my Spring that
will also be.)

# Ranch-Infused Philosophy

It is Spring and Professor Anne Brooks is teaching an Intro-duction to Philosophy/ Metaphysics class at Eastern Oregon State University in La Grande, Oregon. Anne had grown up on a cattle Ranch near a small town, Elgin, Oregon, which is situated twenty miles North of La Grande. The population of La Grande is ap-prox.imately 15,000, while Elgin is only 1500. Anne started her teaching career after raising four children. Due to health problems following a bout with Tetanus when she was thirty years old, she can only teach part time.

The cold, rainy, and windy days, common to the Grande Ronde Valley, delayed the forth coming of Spring until the end of April or May, with occasional snow furies even this late. The class was going well. This cheered Anna along. She had twenty-one students and five of them had some background in Philosophy. The others, of course, did not and it was difficult to get them excited about the grand, historic ideas presented. The five helped with discussions or to move the ideas about, but it seemed this was it. Ideas only. No real enthusiasm or aliveness concerning these notable foundational inspirations.

The first lecture was on the Pre-Socratics. Anne struggled to impute some alive concepts or, rather, important ideas, values and experiences that go beyond concepts. The class was three hours in length, which made it difficult with regard to short attention spans. During the last hour it was apparent that everyone was merely going through the motions, a very unpleasant feeling for Anne.

She was also disappointed at the students' lack of knowledge concerning major Ideas that helped form the Western World. The defining of "Metaphysics" was difficult due to this absence of apperception. She realized that there were indeed many ways of viewing this term. She tried to explain various possibilities without throwing everyone into no man's land where ideas float around as though each one was on a separate journey.

Anna stood in front of the class attempting this feat of an-choring the ideas onto something concrete and passionate. She took a deep breath and said, while pacing back and forth and around and around the room, that Metaphysics can be defined simply as the "Basic Stuff" behind the many, or the multiple appearances of the physical world. The question at stake is what does this reality consist of and how can we know it? And this is leads into the problem of Epistemology. What can know and how we can know it.

Animism was another concept that Anne tried to convey. "This is the idea that the world is a living creature, the life force or movement from the One to the Many inherent in the One, or the "Basic Stuff" that makes up the many things in the world." Anne glanced around the room to see if the students were still awake before proceeding. Don Blackstone who sat in the very last roll was looking up at the ceiling as though something of interest was happening in that region.

"Don," Anne, said loud and especially clear, "What do you feel is the connection between Metaphysics and Animism?"

"Well ah, I think maybe it is the realization that the life force somehow penetrates the physical world in such a way that it is identical with the One behind the Many, that the two co-exist," Don said while looking straight ahead.

"Very good answer," Anne replied, realizing that he had been paying exquisite attention in spite of watching what it was that had been of interest on the ceiling. Turns out, it had been a certain design that had captured his attention. It had depicted a large circle with smaller circles inside, and then he thought he saw yet smaller circles within, and on and on indefinitely. He felt this could reflect what Professor Brooks meant by Metaphysics or a deeper realty within yet another reality. Don was a very creative thinker and if it appeared that he was not paying attention, this was not true. He simply had to make associations for all the input, which was what he had been doing.

Anne continued by describing Thales as the first Philosopher and Critical Thinker who imagined that Water was the One behind the many. Perhaps his reason for this was because water gives life to most things in the world and was a self-moving force. He was followed by Anaxander who disagreed and thought instead that there existed an unbounded substance that was the origin of everything. Anaxames followed Anaxander by making the claim that air was the Primary Substance.

Anne ended the class by giving a short summary of Pythgoras, the Philosopher and Mystic who gave numbers the privilege of being the "Basic Stuff." These numbers also had a Mystical bearing, as did the study of Mathematics and Geometry. Of course, he was also the originator of the Pythagorean Theorem.

The following week Anne was preparing her lecture on the Sophists and Socratics. On Saturday she drove to Elgin to visit her son, A Z for Adam Zackery, who had decided to stay put in Elgin as a cattle rancher, thus keeping up the ranching tradition for the family. Anne's other children were teaching and in business.

She loved to venture out to the small ranch. The ranch house was situated beneath a cliff-like canyon and a small creek called Clark's Creek, which ran through the barnyard across the road from the house. It was a beautiful setting and here Anne could relax and take in the countryside, close to the reality of the earth.

There were always interesting activities going on; horses to be fed, and at times caught for a ride to check on the cattle. She liked to simply watch as her son loaded them into the horse trailer. Ranch house, cows, horses, wide-open spaces, Socrates and the Sophists all seemed to crowd into her thought and imagination. It was as though she had brought Socrates along on the visit, like he was there also seeing what she saw, feeling what she felt.

Of course, Socrates had been in Athens, a city-state in Greece during the 4$^{th}$ century BC., but he surely would have appreciated a day in the country. He was also a mystery, an enigma, Anne thought as she watched her son lead Big Black into the trailer. She could feel the Philosopher's persona or presence, that presence that had intruded upon the souls of many others over the seasons.

While being interrogated by Socrates, people could begin to see the distance between what they were and what they could become. They suddenly understood that they had the potential to become more. In a sense, this is what the famous summons, "to know yourself" is all about. It is recognizing that the inner lower energies have absorbed the higher energies, and the higher energies are evoked through the very presence of Socrates.

Anne smiled to herself as she watched the trailer drive away. She would have liked to go with them, but she could no longer ride much due to her health problems. So, instead, a walk with Socrates down the road to the creek was almost as good. She liked the live experience of ideas concerning Socrates and felt she must include it her lecture next week. Of course, there were many other aspects or things to be said of the Old Gentleman, and where to begin was always the big question.

As she stepped onto the old bridge across the creek, she paused to watch the water flow, which reminded her of the Pre-Socratic Heraclitus who understood we cannot step in the same River twice, as everything is in a state of flux or change. At the same time there is an order, as the world is in complete, perfect balance. This harmony emanates from the Cosmic God or Ultimate Force that is rational as well as experiential in the essence of its nature. Every individual soul is a spark of this divine order, encompassing unity within diversity.

A hawk flew swiftly overhead. Anne turned around and saw its graceful, free-like soaring, gliding on the wind. The creek flowed peacefully through the pasture. Anne stooped over to investigate a small opening, the doorway for a small animal. Life surrounded her everywhere. The universe was alive with abundance and beauty. She smiled, allowing herself to be fully in the moment, while at the same time appreciating the mystery of Socrates and Plato. The idea of the Good appeared, and, indeed she thought, the world is good. Yes, evil exists, but today surrounded by nature's beauty, she saw only the good.

Socrates had a strange way of defining evil as he felt an evil act is committed only from ignorance. If individuals were aware of the great and terrible damage to their souls, they would not commit evil acts. Plus, the supreme Form, The Good, gives life, existence and know-ability to everything in the world. Happiness is not clinging to lesser desires such as success, power or pleasure. It is seeking, knowing, and doing the Good. How marvelous, Anne thought, to adhere to the Good no matter how stupid or inopportune it might appear.

A huge rock or boulder sat beside the creek. It looked like a statue of a huge person leaning over, as though puzzling over the flow of water running over and about. Perhaps, Rodin had stopped here briefly on his way to the other world; not really long enough to complete it, as the call to the Great Beyond was entirely too great. Or, perhaps, he had just wanted to give it a start towards perfection, and then give it back to nature or the elements to complete the task. Anne ambled over and sat upon the awkward figure, feeling grand and good as she too was not as yet completed.

Socrates had been described as a gadfly, since he ignited or evoked a new shape or form signaling the beginning of an inner transformation within individuals. But then he left them incomplete since they themselves needed to learn how to become more aware of the great reality within and without.

"Oh, my God!" Anne cried in vexation. This process surely takes a long time and is never really completed. As Jean Paul Sartre claimed, we are always Being-*for*-itself, never Being-*in*-itself, as are the objects of the world. We are always incomplete, meaning we forever have Absolute Freedom. We have the choice to be something other than what we imagine we are.

Anne's mind continued to contemplate: "I am getting older and I can now begin to understand how all is vanity. However, the Shem Baal Tov, the founder of the Mystical Hasidic tradition in Judaism, felt that it was incorrect to say that all is vanity. God is Good. A Good God created the world as Good, and thus all is not vanity. If we think so, then we do not recognize or realize the Goodness of God's creation."

Today, Anne was not in the mood to take this idea of the Good any further, not now. It was too beautiful here in the country to allow her thoughts to begin their tedious wondering and wandering in the wilderness with the problem of good, evil, and suffering; nor to form a case for justifying the ambiguity of a Good God creating such a world.

She reluctantly left the Rock Man and started for the ranch house. She paused beside the hay stack and watched a group of barn swallows gathering pieces of hay for their nests. Then they flew, one by one or two by two, out towards the barn eves, poking the hay into the soft mud already plastered there. What a grand thing, so grand it is to see these birds at work with the aid of instincts only, or so we have been informed. But then just what is instinct and how much of the stuff do we have, or how many things do we do that are unconscious, not reflecting our incredible ability to think rationally with our 100 billion cranial nerves? In--stincts for animals, and also for us, are built in so we all can survive this great and potently dangerous world.

Of course, it would be better for us humans if we operated more from our basic instinct for survival than the set-up that is occurring now where groups of people are using aspects of our reason and belief systems to justify terrible violence that kills and mains thousands of innocent people. We would be better off like these tiny birds, minding our own business, building nests, and propagating their species without murdering each other or the other birds around them. To be sure Anne had saw two birds of the same species fighting it out on campus a few days ago, a very unusual sight; the good news being that they soon gave it up without injury to either bird.

Plato, in his famous book, *The Republic*, defines one sense of justice as including minding one's own business. This meant in part, that people should know where they belonged in a society according to their talents and aptitudes. Then, in peace and harmony, they should remain where they supposedly belonged. The intent to foster peace and harmony, of course, led to issues of slavery, abuse of power, domination hierarchies, and such, so the Utopia he was attempting to construct could not be actualized. Another problem is that totalitarianism inevitably sneaks in as a variable, or something else miserable that does not and cannot fit into such a tightly knit system.

Anne walked to the house and sat in the yard waiting for the horse group to return. She would then stay for supper and drive home to LaGrande. She sat alongside the house in the sun reading again the allegory of the Cave by Plato, an essay that had been in her blue canvas book bag in the car.

This was not extraordinary as this essay along with The Ring of Gyges and two philosophical text books was always in the car so she could read where she went. Every time she re-read these materials her personal life development enabled her to find a new or more nuanced meanings. Never ending curiosity kept familiar words from becoming stale and out of date.

The pickup with the horse trailer pulled an hour later. She again watched as AZ unloaded Big Black, followed by three other

116

big powerful horses.  AZ looked over and smiled.  He was an exceptionally silent person, almost what one could describe as a contemplative.  And yet, he did not express a belief in God or any other force.  Underneath his silent nature Anne could detect a beautiful thinking, caring mind and soul.

He also possessed a very quiet and unassuming way of being there for others.  He was like the embodiment of the Biblical word: "Do  not let your right hand know what your left hand is doing." Yes, thought Anne, he does belong here on the ranch quietly riding, and working close to nature.  He seems to exist as a child of the Tao, a Taoist hermit.  No attachment to beliefs, theories, or fanfare; just riding the waves of the Tao, the energy and force of God, without adhering to dogma of any sort.  Just "To Be;" is this not the true way of things?

AZ, however, was more talkative than usual during dinner at Timbers, the fancy restaurant in downtown Elgin.  Joyce, his wife was working the late shift at the lumber mill and so it was just Anne and AZ; a real chance to communicate more deeply.

When AZ went to the rest room, Anne wondered what luck she would have when returning to class, trying to communicate the lived experience that gives rise to necessarily abstract philosophical principles.  Could she help build that bridge between the students' authentic life of family, friends, earth, sex, curiosity, movies, food, etc. and the history of philosophy. Could she get them interested in checking out their experiences with those of others in the tradition that came before them, so that a live, rich, ongoing dialogue could be continued into the future?  Could she live with her failure or disappointment, if this was not happening?  How many exceptional students like Don would it take to keep her hanging in there?

## A Walk

Walked up a road
Where the fields and
The trees extend beneath
The cliffs.

A rock of such gigantic
Size caught my notion
And behold, upon this
Stone I now sit.

Below I can see a town, barn, trees, and
The mountains overlooking the
The peaceful scene.

An autumn breeze is gently blowing,
And a magpie is calling its caw outward
For all to hear.

Leaves are red and yellow,
The stubborn ones remain green.
In defiance of winter's coming glare, time
Will tell, and they too will color and
Fall from the tree.

It is strange to sit here over looking this all,
Like an overseer of some important task I feel,
And yet no such thing as that is here.

When across the fields
Over towards the tall
Trees came the loud
Shriek of the hawks.
And behind me a squeaky

Chant belonging to
The insect world.

A task it seems again to me.
A job being done, life's own way
Of completing itself.
And it is all before me now.
To sit and ponder,
Look and see, is like a
Miracle to me.

I must now leave this
Scene and take the
Task of life with me,
And, perhaps, a fulfillment of
Of that life will be.

It will not be a miracle
At all, but what God
Always meant it to be.
Now what a smile
I have with me.

(Oct l974. This poem was written as I sat on my special rock behind
our house on Indian Creek.)

# Leave Taking

Grandmother Meg (Meg to the outside world, Maggie to herself) seemed in a world of her own making, preparing for leave taking. She didn't whisper this secret to the flowers, as the flowers wouldn't understand, nor would the trees. She merely crawled along, pulling weeds and turning over the rich, thick soil. Soil she had fertilized with her leftover table scraps and with manure hauled from her daughter's barnyard. She relished each moment, intent upon caring for each individual flower; no hurry, nowhere to go, as she prepared for her leave taking. Lazy summer days with no need to think as she prepared the flowers, trees, birds, bees and friendly squirrels, her children and grandchildren. Everyone except Willy, her husband; with him the distance had grown too great and had separated them forever. The patterns -- the endless, ruthless patterns of their relationship -- were too embedded, like the roots of the two giant oak trees standing like gladiators in their yard. Her body spoke silently to the plants, like it used to speak to Willy, as she paused awhile beside each one, touching and sniffing the bright open blossoms. She was quiet as each moment was drawn into her, like the air one breathes, and then the moment lingered before sliding and slipping passively, pensively, into the next. Each moment, second, and movement was a blessing. She needed nothing except this recollection of time into the present. Her past seemed remote and dead, its fleeting images and feelings surfacing only occasionally, circling around her like peeping toms.

One evening, she settled herself onto the garden bed just to sit and sift the soil through her fingers, the rich, thick soil, which she had prepared. Willy was indoors watching TV, a favorite position for the aging man. She sat beside her favorite rose bush. The wealthy, deep multi-yellow colors danced with the setting sun, screening and reflecting, circling and consuming. How beautiful it appeared to her; she moved closer -- and, bending forward, she inhaled the blossom. Sweet Fragrance! She held this erotic odor within, allowing it to slowly, carefully, penetrate, as she had once done with the tingly feelings of pleasure after she and Willy had made love. A faint smile gently caressed her face, as though Willy's hand had rested there, like a flicker of light darting across

120

an open doorway, and the peeping toms of her past raced her to the beginnings. Past scenes emerged like water bubbles on a quiet water surface, and then the bubbles exploded, causing tiny ripples to dance, play, and dart across the water, disappearing into the air -- and the water, not dallying, moving, churning, and then vanishing. As each remembrance occurred, she felt the ending gather like autumn leaves into the beginning. She held her hands apart and then brought them together as though in prayer, the left and the right, the beginning and the end. As one bubble appeared and then another on the surface of her consciousness, each recollection came alive, tearing and grabbing. Scenes from childhood bounced rapidly in carefree glee, much like herself now enjoying the immediacy of life. Then her adult life issued forth -- her marriage, her children, the love that she had felt -- it all let loose around her and then she felt the struggle and heartaches, the noise, the clutter and the clamor, and as she moved her head *away* from the rose, she felt the joys and pain of her early marriage. Willy had soon begun to control and dominate, and she had allowed him to turn on her space. How weak she was! But she shrugged these thoughts away as the recollection bubble burst, escaping without care into the atmosphere. Love gone wrong, all the terrible human frailties, hers and Willy's -- and with an extended sigh she placed her cupped hands slightly, gently, over the rose, holding the hands there as in tribute. Nothing but nothing seemed to matter. "Oh," she thought, "what long, glorious, lazy summer days." Her hands flew from the rose, parting the air momentarily, and moved into the rich, thick, soil. She dug down with long, bony fingers, capturing the earth, and then began to rub the tiny leftover particles between her finger tips.

She could faintly hear noise from the TV; it reminded her of the rattle and clutter of unlived life, and she wondered if she had escaped this grey, deadly trap. Perhaps she had escaped, but then why was she still with Willy? Nothing, nothing really mattered now. Nothing could really be understood; there were no "whys" and "ifs," only the lazy summer days, like "ole engine 99 going down the railroad line, going nowhere and everywhere."

Willy's loud voice broke the silence: "It's late, aren't you coming?" Walking around the corner of the house he saw her and continued, "What are you doing, returning to your childhood?

121

You're acting like a baby, crawling around, playing in the dirt." He then added, with a slight upward twist of his mouth, "Get in, what will the neighbors think?" He helped her struggle to gain support since her legs were stiff and weak, and as she rose the dirt granules fell downward, rejoining the soil. Will tugged at Meg's blouse sleeve, urging her to hurry into their bungalow so she would be hidden from the world. Once inside he slammed shut the door and shouted, "Damn it, woman, you aren't senile, so why do you act so foolishly? Do you think you can get away with it because you are old? Sitting out there in the flower bed talking to your roses. I'll bring one inside and you can talk to it or admire it or whatever, inside where the neighbors can't see." As he said this, he banged through the door and soon returned with the multi-colored yellow rose. "There!" he shouted. Then, lowering his voice as though he was a lover. "Here is your rose." Placing it in a vase with water, he quickly gave it to her. A slight grimace darted across his face as though he too had remembered something from the past. Meg looked away as sadness suddenly consumed her. But, as she turned carrying the vase, the sorrow vanished and was swept away as quickly as it had appeared. Nothing seemed to matter, as she felt whole and alive. So, perhaps love had not really gone wrong. Upon entering her bedroom, she felt her heart beating rapidly as though she had just finished a footrace and her breath was forced, jerky and in short gasps. Her heart was giving up and she knew it -- the slow, lazy summer days were like her ebbing pulse, slowly moving like ole engine 99, going somewhere and nowhere, down the railroad line.

She placed the rose on her bedside stand and sat on the bed staring at its stark loveliness, not thinking of how it had really come to be there. She was suddenly too tired to get up. Her body felt heavy, like lead, and her arms and legs seemed to be detaching themselves from her torso. She leaned back on the pillow and, closing her eyes, she saw the rose floating in the darkness of her inner world. It tossed and turned under dark rolling clouds.

This inner scene did not exclude hearing Willy in the adjoining bedroom preparing for bed. She remembered his young taut body. He seemed so vital then, with hard, coarse muscles that she had loved to caress; she had felt the energy there and had held him tight, touching and loving. She now saw his old narrow body; he would be leaning naked over the old black walnut dresser reaching for his pajama bottoms. He wore the bottoms without the tops. She saw his thin bony shoulders with the loose skin pulled downward, like smooth rolling hills. His hips and thighs were no longer firm, but like his shoulders, the skin sagged and pulled as though determined to undress him. The rose image spun around Willy's nakedness, as though touching him for the last time. She thought she heard Willy sit on the bedside, an old habit of his. He would sit and then swing both legs up onto the bed while lowering his head and shoulders onto the pillow and mattress. She had watched him do this many time the first years of their marriage while snuggling into her corner of the bed. Then he would reach over and caress her gently, running his hand down and around her eager body. But soon the swinging onto the bed and even the touching became habitual, mere functional habits. Will had not remembered that a person, Maggie, lived there under the smooth, rounded, sensuous skin.

The rose image grew dimmer, evaporating into Maggie's inner eye as she pulled the colorful afghan around her coldness. She was too tired to slip into bed; her body seemed heavy. Turning on her side, she listened for Willy's coarse snore, waiting there for nothingness. Stillness overcame the room like a breeze brushing against the trees, Meg's head twisted slightly as she again thought she felt Willy's hand touching her face.

Meg's daughter, Liz, arrived early the next morning and, seeing her mother's condition, she called the doctor and her sister, Sandy. Maggie had remained in bed staring sometimes at the rose and then into space, as though preparing her sight for the great reckoning -- or whatever it was to be. Her breaths were forced, painful, uneven jerks, and a hot burning pain was consuming her chest. Willy sat watching an early morning talk show. When Liz told him about Meg, he answered without moving his eyes form the set.

"She's alright, just upset with me. She'll come around before noon. But I tell you she ain't right in the head anymore."

Liz didn't answer, she had grown up with the sparks of her parents' relationship and had decided long ago to ignore it all. Walking into the bedroom she stood beside the bed, sadly looking at Meg. The tired woman smiled up at her.

"Don't be so sad, none of us can live forever, it will be alright. Did you call Sandy?"

"Yes, she will soon be here."

Meg seemed relieved as she sank further into her haven, the pillow, which surrounded her head as though to comfort and lighten her burden.

"Isn't the yellow rose a real beauty? I would love to enter one of them in the county fair," Meg uttered between short jerky gasps. Liz nodded and looked away. The rose seemed an almighty intruder that she didn't like.

Sandy appeared in the doorway with her usual friendly smile and greeting." Good morning all. Mom aren't you well?" she asked, reaching over and kissing Maggie on the forehead. "You'll be fine soon. Just rest today, and you'll be fine tomorrow. What a fine rose. Did you pick it from your garden?"

Maggie nodded and attempted to respond, but her heavy body and light limbs were at odds. "What a strange pair," she thought and again struggled to tell Sandy that Willy had given her the rose. It seemed important that she should know. Finally, "No, your father gave it to me."

"Dad! Now isn't that a surprise!" Sandy said, not wanting to continue.

Maggie returned to the task at hand -- breathing. So difficult, an unconscious habit of necessity all her life and now such agony and effort. The chest pain felt like hot burning iron pressing relentlessly, grudgingly, hatefully against her ribs. Yes, her body was at odds with her inner self and she didn't know how to reconcile the two. She felt the smoothness of the lazy summer days, rolling, rolling along like ole engine 99 going down the railroad line, going nowhere and everywhere. It didn't matter, no it didn't matter that her body was heavy, her limbs light, her breathing no longer easy, easy, nice and easy. "Why," she thought to herself, "no one even thinks about breathing, it just is, it just happens. No, it doesn't matter, nothing, nothing and nothing, that's all there is" she said to herself as the hot demons struck her in the chest.

Why should it please her so? Such nonsense! How could this be? Surely there is something, always there is something, goings on and comings on, people crying, people laughing, people making love, eating, working, and on and on and on, always something. Yes, there was plenty going on, plenty. An even deeper hot jab yanked through her, making her whine -- not cry out, but whine -- and then to shut out the pain forever and ever she began to think about the rose. The multi-colored yellow rose, so tender she felt it was, and now it too would die. Yes, it too would die because Willy had plucked it from its stem. Its fate to perish and no longer greet the sun, rather than to dance and reflect the sunset. "You and I are in the same sort of fix, Mr. or Mrs. Rose, whatever you might be, yessiree." "Yessiree," she continued, "we are certainly in a bind, but it will be fine because I have a secret." She turned her head slightly on her private haven and winked at the rose. "I might name you something special, really special, because you are a special rose and we are comrades in distress."

The pain again awakened her, and she uttered another whine -- quietly, ever so quietly. She could hear Liz and Sandy discussing the situation. "What situation?" she asked herself. "I am dying, that's what." Evidently, from what she could piece together, they had decided to call an ambulance as her doctor wanted her in the hospital immediately. Little did they know that she and the rose were now close companions, both waiting for the finale, whatever it was to be.

Her worn, bony hands flung hopelessly upon her equally bony chest, "The pain, oh, the goddamn pain," she muttered to herself. "There isn't a name for you, though," she thought, coveting the rose with her eyes and her being. "You exist alone, but you also exist symbolically for each person. What glorious symbols we humans have pushed on to your loveliness -- love, beauty, truth."

She released her hold on the rose as though reckoning that in truth its beauty was only an illusion concocted with mighty human ideals. In her situation she found it difficult to feel any of these super-minded apparitions. Her head twisted slightly away from her new found nameless friend and she was filled with the laziness of slow-moving summer days.

The ambulance driver and attendant expertly moved Maggie onto the stretcher. Her famous carriage was awaiting. She remembered Emily Dickinson's famous poem

"Because I could not stop for Death" and silently ran a few lines through and out of herself:

125

The Carriage held but just Ourselves --
and Immortality.
We slowly drove -- He knew no haste
And I had put away
My labor and my leisure too,
For His Civility --
We passed the School where Children strove
At Recess -- in the Ring --
We passed the Fields of Gazing Grain,
We passed the Setting Sun --

Liz and Sandy stood beside Willy, who watched the pro-
ceedings wordlessly. Once or twice it seemed he opened his
mouth to speak but shaking his head he closed his mouth tight
and then turned to the green overstuffed haven of his chair as
Meg was wheeled out their front door. "She'll be fine, I should
know, shouldn't I?  Just one of those anxiety attacks" he said,
leaning back into his haven as all his senses covetously surrounded the TV set.

The ambulance driver had shut the door and was starting the
engine as everything was in order for the journey, when he heard
Meg's voice ring in strong and firm: "Please raise me up -- I want
to take one last look at my town as I go along." The driver glanced
back and watched the attendant prop Maggie up so she could see
out. She was pleased -- and in between the jerky breaths she
muttered something that sounded like, "That's fine," or "that's
nice," and then again she spoke in a strong clear voice: "I can now
see where I re-walked all these years -- downtown, uptown, nowhere and everywhere -- past the trees, the flowers, buildings,
people, the corner grocery -- and now we go past the sun." Her
voice caught and was lost deep in her chest as she struggled for
air.

At the hospital, two nurses appeared and took command,
Maggie was now in their keeping. She felt powerless, helpless and
uncomfortable as the two white strangers pushed her further
onward.

Liz and Sandy had no sooner entered the emergency entrance when the tallest of the two nurses handed Liz Maggie's
purse and, in a business-like tone of voice, instructed her to check

126

Meg in at the front desk and then wait in her mother's room, as the doctor had ordered x-rays. Liz and Sandy then entered what seemed a stark, cold room. Liz shivered as she placed Meg's purse on the bed stand. Sandy pulled back the top sheet and poked the pillow with her fists in hopes of softening it for her mother.

Within a few minutes the nurse returned and without emotion announced Meg's death: "She died on the x-ray table; it was so sudden, there was nothing we could do." She said this as though announcing that dinner was on the table.

The x-ray table had been cold, remote, unfriendly and hard for Maggie. It had been a shock. She could not sink her head into a soft haven or glance at the bedside rose. All earthly comforts were gone. "Why have they done this?" she had thought to herself. "' Can't they, don't they know what is happening? No, how can they? Because people are always dying here, coming in or going out."

She was so tired, so weary of fighting, of struggling for air, it was so strange to have to fight for something that had once been so natural. She let out the trapped air -- but then refused to struggle for another. It was too much effort here on the cold stark table. Thinking of the slab she was on, she shivered, and tiny hot irons racked her chest, but then her heavy body no longer felt like iron. Her body had become light enough to meet her arms and legs and she let go -- she just relaxed, refusing to struggle any longer.

How good it was to finally let go, to release herself completely. She turned to tell the nurse this, in that split second between life and death, but the words were swallowed up. It was too late. She was marching past the sun. "Oh," she thought to herself, "the lazy slow-moving summer days, going nowhere and everywhere." Then she saw the stain on the front of the tall nurse's meticulous uniform. The spot was in fact a mere discolored area about an eighth of an inch in diameter. That was all. So minute, so small -- and Maggie saw it. As she sank into her death she smiled because the stain was surely invisible to everyone except herself. How wonderful it had been, how very splendid to have been summoned down, down, and then up and up -- and then it was all stain, all rose, all everything and all nothing.

The ambulance driver was again summoned in his winged chariot to transport Meg's body away from the living, to hide it away forever. It was as though Willy was tugging and pulling her inside.

"It's darn hard to believe that only 45 minutes ago she was lifted up to see her town," said the driver as he wheeled the occupied cart out the large double doors. The door shut securely behind them.

Willy, when told the news, had asked his daughters to leave, as he had wanted to be alone to think of the dead. He walked into Meg's room and, seeing the multi-colored yellow rose, had stared at it as though it was an unknown demon. He then sank onto the bed, emitting a heavy, coarse sigh. He was, however, too tired to swing his legs up. So, with great effort, he reached downward using his hand and arms, and helped lift his legs up and over.

With another deep leveling sigh, he stretched out upon the bed. His body felt heavy and he was cold. He pulled the colorful afghan up around himself and snuggled into the hollow left there by Meg's body. He clung to this space as though she was still there to feel and caress him. Shadows of tears touched upon his face and gripped him, not letting go. The deed was done, life was no more, the leave taking was complete.

# Essays

# "Leave Taking" and Heidegger

by

## Patricia Herron
## with Steven Bindeman

**Author notes:** See Professor Herron's author note at the end of the volume. Steven L. Bindeman, until his retirement in Dec. 2010, was Professor of Philosophy and Department Chairperson at Strayer University, Arlington campus. His teaching experience reflects not only his interest in philosophy and psychology, but in film and media studies, science fiction, world music, and comparative religion. He has been elected into *Who's Who in American Colleges and Universities*. He has published articles on Heidegger, Wittgenstein, Levinas, the creative process, and postmodernism, alongside numerous book reviews. His first book, *Heidegger and Wittgenstein: The Poetics of Silence* (Lanham: University Press of America, 1981) is currently listed as a recommended text under the listing "Heidegger" in the *Encyclopedia Britannica*. He recently published a second book, *"The Anti-Philosophers"* (Peter Lang, 2015), and his third, *"Silence and Postmodernism"* is currently in search of a publisher. Communication concerning this article may be addressed to bindeman1@verizon.net

In preparing this work for publication Dr. Bindeman did some editing of Prof. Herron's story, and expanded on her Heideggerian reflection on it.

# Abstract:

"Leave Taking" is a short story about an elderly woman's reflections on the meaning of her life as she experiences its final hours. She considers the growing distance between her pragmatic husband Willy and herself while she spends time in her garden, contentedly digging in the soil, enjoying her roses along with her connection to all of nature. Her death comes upon her suddenly, yet naturally. The story is followed by a series of confrontations with key concepts from the works of Martin Heidegger that are used to further explore themes introduced in the story. His thoughts on the essential nature of thinking as thanking are considered, along with his analysis of time and being, the fourfold, and his belief that life is a gift that we should learn to embrace rather than to reject.

**Keywords:** Heidegger; death and dying; Being of beings; the fourfold

## Part I: "Leave Taking" (above)

## Part II: "Leave Taking" and Martin Heidegger

Martin Heidegger in his book *What is Called Thinking?* describes what he feels is the essential nature of thinking. In that work, he writes that "Joyful things, too, and beautiful and mysterious and gracious things give us food for thought. These things may even be more thought-provoking than all the rest ..." (Heidegger, 1968, 51).

These things, he adds, are a gift which we should keep in mind so as not to reject it (51). The contemplation of such joyful things is a form of joyful thinking -- and such thinking is a kind of *thanking* (Heidegger, 1965, 49).

Heidegger also says that we need to learn how to let things be (see Heidegger, "Dialogue on a Country Path," 1966, x). In "Leave Taking," I have touched upon these notions in order to exhibit how this mode of thinking explains death. In order to understand how essential thinking deals with death it is necessary to understand that due to our essential participation in the world, it is possible both to reveal our individual uniqueness and to recognize the uniqueness of particular beings.

The particularity that embraces both the person and particular beings is, in "Leave Taking," present during the life of Maggie, and is present in the same manner when Maggie is exposed to the final reality of her own death. This parallel, I feel, between our essential participation in the world and our approach to death is a natural phenomenon through which our perception of particular beings exhibits an unfolding of everything and nothing.

When Maggie thinks to herself, "How very splendid to be summoned down, down, and then up, up and then it was all stain,

132

all rose, all everything and all nothing," these lines implicitly denote this relationship between death and the essential nature of our thinking, which is simply a kind of thinking that allows particular beings to exist in their particularity: the rose is, the stain is, death is and Maggie is.

This essentiality also reflects a person's own particularity and cannot be avoided when he or she is exposed to the final reality of death. We die alone; no one can die for us. We might reach out with our public natures, herd understanding, or ideal of "socialized man" to help us die, but it won't work. We die alone, exposed to our own nothingness.

Within this particularity of the self, which also allows a particular being to be that which it is as a being, exists the unfolding of the everything and nothing spoken of in "Leave Taking." Meaning occurs only through our special manner of participation in the world, derived from our experiencing of "things" in the world.

Death cannot be experienced; only the dying is experienced; therefore, death has no meaning since it is not part of our essentiality. We can speak of nothingness as the cessation of life or speak of nothingness, non-being and negation, as the absence of "things" in a dialectical sense. We can say that life is, and that nothingness or death is the opposite of what we know life to be.

It can be inferred then, that meaning begins and ends with our understanding of things in the world. We understand these things because of their essential difference from other things. There are many examples. For instance, we only know cold because we experience heat. If all "things" in the world were green, we would not know colors, or even know the green surrounding us.

The nothingness, therefore, that I speak of in "Leave Taking" is not the mere concept of nothingness derived from our experiences. Instead, this nothingness is the void prior to thought and as such cannot be spoken of or understood. *We only know that it is there.*

It cannot be spoken of because we cannot determine the foundation for meaning from what already has meaning. In other words, since we must have thought before we can have meaning, we cannot speak of this void within language and thought.

On the other hand, this nothingness that has no name (Maggie also did not name the rose; she left it nameless) is

133

intrinsic to the essential nature of thinking. This is the case because without the perceiving and thinking that reveals particular beings and without specific beings showing their faces, there would be nothing. But instead there is everything. Everything and nothing -- how very close we always are to the abyss of nothingness.

The mystery of death also cannot be spoken of since it cannot be experienced. In this manner, death represents the unspoken nothingness paralleling the abyss of nothingness present within our essential participation with the world. But, instead, there is everything.

In "Leave Taking," I have touched upon this extreme paradox of everything and nothing. Necessary and coupled with this unfolding into the dichotomy of everything and nothing, is a sense of particular beings, or what Heidegger (in *Being and Time*, 1962, 49; also in *What is Called Thinking?*, 1966, 242)) calls the Being of beings, i.e., our ability to think particular beings, but only in relation to our concepts or universal ideas which exist unchanged in the past, present and future.

In this manner, memory does not consist of mere memory of facts, data, or past events, but rather, memory of Being, or all that is. In this thinking, time and being are one and the same and, likewise, thought and being are one and the same. This idea reflects Heidegger's concept of time in *Being and Time* and is in opposition to the Aristotelian "now" of time.

This means that In Aristotelian thinking, being exists only in "pure presence." This "pure presence" transcends the temporal world and is present only in the now, while the past is no longer, and the future is not yet; thus, for Aristotle past and future do not participate in "pure presence."

Being in this manner is placed in a timeless eternal realm, while particular beings remain in the world of flux. (See Heidegger, 1962, 48.) This notion of two sites for the "Being of beings" is also present in Platonic thinking and will be discussed later.

In order for particular beings to participate in Being, and for Being to participate in particular being, it is necessary for thought to transcend particular being only so that particular being can be that which it, as a being, is.

134

In *What is Called Thinking?* Heidegger used a statement from the writings of Parmenides, a Greek thinker who lived around the turn of the sixth century B.C.: "One should both say and think that Being is" (Heidegger, 1968, 178). Heidegger analyzed this saying by changing it into the following, "It is useful to let-lie-before-us and so the taking-to heart also: being in being" (Heidegger, 1968, 223). These two sayings will be used in order to analyze Maggie's essential nature of thinking.

In contrast to essentiality, there is a mode of "being in the world" that avoids essentiality. Humans in this mode participate in what I have termed the "totality of all that is," or with a general attitude toward the world. In this general attitude, either there is no correspondence to the is-ness of specific beings or there exists a denial of being.

In essential thinking however there exists a closing of the gap between being and life. Maggie's world is present to her in a certain special way, present to both her heart and mind. Willy in contrast fears his own emptiness and, therefore, desires to create external "things" to compensate for the inward void. Willy yields to these "things," not as things in themselves like with Maggie's attitude toward the world, but in a mode of generality. He focuses on his things because he does not want to feel the nothingness of his own emptiness, the nothingness that is intrinsic to essential thinking.

In order to avoid the nothingness that surrounds his perception of "things," a nothingness that has also become part of his nature due to his lost sense or denial of Being, Willy seeks refuge in an attitude that encompasses a whole. While his wholeness is an attitude of people in general, it is not real. Willy's attitude toward the world, therefore, resembles the mode of the "totality of all that is," while Maggie's life reflects the essential nature of thinking.

Maggie's connectedness with her world stage lends itself to her in death. It is as though Death is, the rose is, and the stain is, all existing in the same presencing, and thus, along with her, we are permitted a brief glimpse of the "something" that is essential to thinking while we also participate in death's ambiguity.

The tone and setting in the story add to these dimensions of understanding death. These devices, like the contrast between

135

the images of rose and stain are, however, only tools used in the hope of illuminating the "core problematic," which is the essential nature of thinking confronting Maggie as she herself faces death. In that split second between life and death -- what then?

The mystery remains veiled and I turn to Emily Dickinson, who also attempted an inside view of death; this is especially evident in her poem "Because I Could Not Stop for Death," a poem that is alluded to in "Leave Taking," in which Dickinson announces that only the ambiguity of death can be realized.

In the very first setting of the story we find Maggie sitting in her garden. This setting is crucial because it sets the stage for her confrontation with the essential nature of thinking. It is also in this setting that we encounter glimpses of the conflict between Willy and Maggie.

In Maggie's perception of the world, there is evidence of "something" that reflects essential thinking, and this illuminating "something" essentiality takes place in the presencing of particular beings in time. The curtain is now raised, and we can imagine ourselves sitting with Maggie. We can listen quietly to the silent dialogue between her and her surroundings, inwardly making things understood in a narrative sequence as it becomes our story, too.

Maggie sits in her flower garden, her world's stage, and feels close to the flowers, the birds, insects, and the soil. She is in a pensive mood and desires to gather her stage toward her in her leave taking. She brings the contents of her garden to heart, she gathers it within her, within her thinking that transcends particular beings only in order that this transcendence may represent the particular being in that which it, as a being, is.

Heidegger too speaks of "gathering." In his essay "The Thing" (in *Poetry, Language, Thought*, 1971, 165-174) he gives the example of a jug, whose essential nature as container cannot be defined completely or objectively in terms of the void it holds. Not until it is seen in terms of what it gives -- namely wine or water, as the gift of drink from its divine source to mortals, does it reveal itself. In the gift of its outpouring, the jug brings together what Heidegger calls in his essay "The Thing" "the fourfold" (173), namely earth and sky, divinities and mortals. "This manifold-simple gathering is the jug's presencing," he adds (174).

136

Maggie's world is present to her in this same special way: present to her heart and mind and to her very being. She allows and sees everything, every being on her stage, as essential. She thus permits everything to remain in its essential nature and she reaches out to touch all in farewell. Maggie does not create a dichotomy between the object and herself, because within her essential nature of thinking, a particular being returns to that which it, as a being, is. For Maggie, being and thought are one and the same. Therefore, in this sense there is no duality. The only duality is the thinking, or the transcending that is necessary for particular being to be that which it is.

She both states and thinks that being is. She states in the manner of letting-lie-before-her being. This is a rose. The rose participates as a rose. It is present and Maggie also takes the rose to heart. Taking it to heart means she gathers the rose to her thinking but releases it again so it can return to its is-ness or its particularity. She treasures this "something" that is her essential nature of thinking. The stating and the saying are interrelated; objects could not show their faces to us without this conjunction of stating and saying.

Maggie states in order to deliver what is present into presence. The words, the stating, the letting-lie-before-her, all lend substance by bringing objects to stand, i.e., to stand within the light where they can be what they are. The statement by Parmenides, "One must both state and say that being is" can be seen as necessary to both thought and particular beings. The stating and thinking and saying are separate and yet they are wholly interrelated.

Maggie is thankful for her essential nature because it is a call of language -- a call that brings "everything" to her -- a call that remains in her memory. Perhaps a poem will somewhat unmask the meaning of this memory that unfolds into time:

I walk along the forest trail
Leaving trees back behind
Meeting new trees all the time.
On either side the forest spreads.
There it lies before me
But by my choosing.

137

All the trees I left behind
Are there still,
And all the trees that I go to meet
Have been waiting there
Upon my trail.
Time is but
Past trees, present trees,
And future trees.
All the trees myself surround.

Maggie also relishes each moment, intent upon caring for each individual flower. She reaches out to her world lying before her, speaking silently to the plants, like her body used to speak to Willy. The rose shows its face in the duality of the stating and thinking and yet returns to that which it is within the duality. It is, as such, both a particular rose and, at the same time, is participating in being because Maggie takes it to heart.

We do not need to understand or do anything else about this essential duality. Maggie both thinks and states that the rose is; the rose is in her memory, or rather, she carries its presence in her memory. With regards to the poem "I walk along the forest trail," "leaving trees behind" can mean leaving trees in one's memory and yet meeting new trees all the time. For Maggie, the trees are present in the past and future in the same way she allows particular beings to remain in their essential being within the present.

Being is brought to light within Maggie`s essential nature of thinking, and this participation is the same in all three modes of time. The trees are present in both the past and future, and are present to the memory by one's choosing, or held there within one's choosing. "All the trees I left behind" are there still, as are "all the trees I go to meet", and there is but *this time*, with its past, present and future all contained within it, where "all the trees surround myself."

There are important differences between how Maggie and Willy relate to the world. Maggie's memory does not merely recall formulated information; her memory can be described also as a "thanking" for her essential nature, which is thinking. She is thankful and, consequently, does not allow her ideas and language to manipulate and change the world.

138

Willy, in contrast, does not think; he merely possesses things and covers the world with his ideas and then declares that these ideas are real since they describe what is meaningful to him. Since Willy must create external things to compensate for his inward void, he remembers in the same way. For example, his memory is dominated by the recalling of facts, data, and events relating to information-gathering. These "things," which constitute an overall attitude, a lack of curiosity with regards to intellectual knowledge, have been placed by him into neat packages, waiting for an opportune time to be opened.

This kind of information-gathering contains both a general attitude and a more precise scientific direction, however. The latter is an especially important factor in the way all of us relate to the world, since it plays a key role in the adding of new insights and inventions that are beneficial for creating a higher standard of living.

Maggie too is part of this functional, intellectual and scientific world, as is every human. Although it might initially appear otherwise, these two approaches to "being-in-the-world" are not examined in this essay in terms of one transcending the other. Rather, they are recognized as being two essential dimensions of meaning-acquisition, co-existing in actual everyday existence; as such, they need to be recognized as necessarily interrelated.

I will therefore refer to the contrast or conflict between Willy and Maggie as occurring most significantly within the confines of their marital enclosure. Within this enclosure, due to their separate attitudes, I will also place their attitudes into two different sites. These sites, however, are interrelated and cannot, in essence, be separated.

Maggie cannot touch Willy in her leave taking. She can reach out to others on her stage, her grandchildren, daughters and friends, but not Willy. Their relationship has become fixed, or too deeply rooted, like the roots of the old oak tree. She can sit in the flower garden enclosure and feel close to the life surrounding her. She can reach out with her essential nature with heart and mind to these surroundings and to the others who participate purely and simply with their own essential natures.

She would not sit in the garden if the flowers had wilted; she would not desire to relate to such a world. In like manner, she cannot speak to or touch Willy's spirit. The distance between them is too great; it is as though they are in two different worlds. Their performing patterns are present only to bridge the gap separating them. Maggie is forced to relate to Willy with his own mode of generality. He doesn't understand anything else. She cannot touch upon his essential nature of thinking. Thus, the marital enclosure resembles a flower garden of wilted flowers: life is gone; it has fled, and Maggie cannot recapture its natural flow.

Past scenes emerge like water bubbles on a quiet water surface, and then the bubbles explode, causing tiny ripples to dance, play and dart across the water. This recollection of the past is not merely a remembrance of events that she retains, in order to recall at her convenience. Her past is part of her, part of her being. It moves and changes her. Her past is not present, like Willy's memory, merely as something to recall, for the purpose of bringing back events to talk and fret over, where only the faculties of the mind are utilized. Her past, as part of her, passes gently like a breeze through her, appearing on the surface and then disappearing, and reappearing and disappearing once again. With each memory she feels the ending, gathered like autumn leaves into the beginning.

Her long bony fingers capture the soil; how she loves the earth, her rose, and then she hears the sounds within the home and a sadness overcomes her. Love gone wrong; she was weak; she had clung to a dead relationship. She releases these thoughts, as nothing, nothing really matters now. Nothing can be understood, there are no "whys" and "ifs." Only the long summer days, like "ole engine 99, going down the railroad line, going nowhere and somewhere."

Maggie's thoughts return to the marital enclosure as she hears the sounds from the television. Willy's life resembles the television drama because he is a spectator; he looks out upon the world from a distance, as a process, not allowing or permitting the particularity of things and experiences to penetrate beyond his intellect.

Maggie admits that she is weak; she has clung to a dead relationship; she has gone through the motions, like someone reciting prayers or performing rituals in hope of bridging the gap between heaven and earth. But she now releases these thoughts,

140

because nothing really matters now. The engine 99 imagery depicts a train that travels between two destinations. The train schedule remains the same, forward to one destination only to return to the other. Back and forth, always going somewhere, and yet going nowhere.

Camus's *Myth of Sisyphus* resembles this motion of going nowhere and somewhere as Sisyphus pushes the rock up down the hill for all eternity. Maggie does not linger in the past or fret over her mistakes. She realizes she is human and, therefore, weak. She neither judges, nor evaluates these past actions, but returns to the lazy summer days, enjoying her world, expecting to go nowhere and yet somewhere. The everywhere and nowhere parallels the up, up and down, down evident in the death scene.

We encounter the marital conflict in the garden setting. Maggie's body speaks to the plants as it used to speak to Willy when she inhales the blossom and holds the erotic odor there as she once held the tingly feelings of pleasure following their love making. But she can no longer touch upon or communicate her attitude or state of "being in the world" to Willy. She cannot bid him farewell.

The marital enclosure is uncomfortable, not like the garden setting, and yet we are led, down, down into the face of it. She cannot reach or touch upon Willy's nature because she exists in an essentiality that closes the gap between being and life while Willy's attitude toward the world broadens this same gap. It is as though they exist apart, in two different sites.

Maggie remembers when this was not the case, when at the beginning of their relationship they could relate, with both mind and body. But love had gone wrong. She doesn't attempt to discover the reason. She only knows that Willy "had not remembered that a person, Maggie, lived there under the smooth rounded, sensuous skin." She had been gathered into Willy's formidable "whole" where particular beings coexist, while "others" are lost in the yawning nothingness of generality.

The marital patterns are also nothing, but they are deeply-rooted, supporting the marital enclosure, compensating for the movement into different sites. These patterns are like rituals or formal prayers repeated over and over. Empty words, empty thoughts, recapitulated in a desperate hope of bridging the gap between them.

Willy is unaware; it is as though he looks upon the world and upon Maggie and cannot bring them into his being. Maggie, on the other hand, is aware of the separation; she sees the beauty of Willy, both as he was in the past and the way he is in the present. "He seemed so vital then, hard coarse muscles that she had loved to caress: she had felt the energy there and had held him tight, touching and loving." "The rose image spun around Willy's nakedness as though touching him for the last time."

So, Maggie did touch Willy, one last time, but only in her thoughts. It is as though she saw his beauty but being separated from him there in time, she could not bring him into her own being, and she grieved over this loss. It is a real, in-depth, sorrow that is as much a part of her as are the trees, flowers, and insects.

In order to remain together, they participated totally in the routine of living, within certain constructed linguistic and action patterns. Maggie knew her role as wife and did her duty: she cooked, cleaned, washed and engaged in appropriate conversations with Willy. Willy's world revolved around these rituals or patterns. He had no other substance, only these external "things."

Maggie's attitude toward the world reflects the essential nature of thinking, and Willy's does not. Maggie has touched upon the "something" that is essential to our thinking, but it still remains vague just what this "something" is. We can discern that it relates to our essential participation within the world and time. We can understand that the presence of particular being takes place within a duality, but a duality that remains hidden. We cannot see or capture this duality, either, not with our senses nor with our intellect.

Our essential nature, thinking, meets the face of particular beings. Then and only then does language become "the house of Being." (See Heidegger, "The Way to Language," in *On the Way to Language,* 135.) This call of particular being toward Being or essential thinking pervades the foundation of metaphysics, and the question persists: what is the particular being in Being?

The early Greeks, however, did not give further thought to the nature of the duality of beings and Being. Plato's interpretation of this duality has persisted in Western-European thinking. According to Plato, it is the idea, the thought or concept, that is the face

142

whereby a given something shows its form or looks at us. Thus, this idea or form constitutes the Being of a being.

If this is the case, then we never look at a rose in its particular being. But rather, we go beyond the immediate rose to the real, and the real being is the form of the idea that is interposed between the object and ourselves. In this manner, particular beings are at once removed from us.

In "Leave Taking," Maggie's essential thinking does not exist in this beyond, because it is only within thought that the object is allowed to be that which it is. Plato's metaphysical duality, a distinction derived from thought, does not however actually place particular beings and Being into two different sites -- there remains but one world.

Likewise, the face of death, like the face of the rose and the stain, is delivered to Maggie within itself, or is exposed to itself in the nakedness of its existence. The stain is seen by Maggie in its particularity, and Maggie's own particularity is also present.

The essential nature of her thinking parallels the is-ness of death. She is not "one" with the totality of all that is, or with "others." Instead, she alone must face the face of death in the same manner that she faces and is faced by particular beings.

Before continuing with the death scene, it is expedient to again examine the marital setting and the rose. This is important because further analysis will expose the difference between participation in the "one" or the "totality of all that is" evident in Willy's attitude, and Maggie's projection towards the is-ness of Being and particular beings.

The rose is also a symbol for their lost love. Willy seems to remember this as he gives the rose to Maggie. "'There!' he shouted; then, lowering his voice as though he were a lover, 'Here is your rose.'" He lowers his voice into a gentle loving tone so different from the "There!" he had just shouted.

Willy does not take the rose to heart, nor does he see Maggie in her uniqueness. He is removed there in time. He does not permit himself to participate in his own essential nature of thinking. His thinking is like the two sites constructed by Plato.

The real site for Plato consists of the forms or the ideas that consume beings and make them into general abstractions. In this theory love became so universalized that love for a particular person could hardly be realized. While Willy's thinking did not embrace the theory of forms, he had, however, lost or had denied to himself any awareness of the uniqueness of people. He remains lost in generality, never realizing -- never, ever knowing that beneath the winter limbs there is life, which, in the spring, will burst into song. But Maggie places her hands on the limbs and feels the bursting into joy.

Willy is angry with Maggie for sitting in the garden. He wants to hide her away. He is embarrassed because she is different. He thinks she is becoming senile and he doesn't want this to be known to the neighbors.

On Willy's stage, essential participation in the world is different from Maggie's, where such participation reflects being and thought. Willy's participation in the world distorts being; he does violence to the essential nature of thinking. He removes himself from this nature and manipulates his world in order to talk, see, learn and do.

As was previously mentioned, both modes of being in the world are dimensions of meaning that co-exist in actual "everyday" existence and as such are necessarily interrelated. It is just that in Willy's thinking everyone moves on the same level of generality without trying to get to the foundation of what is. This kind of participation in the world is one that is removed from the "is-ness" of particular beings.

Willy behaves toward the world as though with a time schedule, like the time schedule for trains where everything must be done in such and such a manner, and at such and such a time. But Maggie is in time only as time allows everything to lend itself in its presence. She claps her hands together and listens to the beat of time; listens, listens, as time speaks the unspoken language.

Language also dominates Willy's world differently than it does in Maggie's world. In his world language creates a dichotomy between subject and object. This is a language that does violence to the world as it gathers everything into a totality that represents everyone and everything as being all clumped together into a single whole.

In Maggie's world on the other hand, language is the means for letting things be. It is the house of Being because it lets things determine their own specific nature.

The rose, the mighty rose as a symbol of truth, love and beauty, becomes a symbol for Maggie's lost love. She releases the rose in her leave-taking, releases it into its essential nature. "You are nameless, you do not have a name."

She realizes that there exists something else, something that reaches further than our lofty sentiments and ideals represented by our traditional and religious symbols. She has tapped into this something, which is really nothing, and she is aware of its treasure.

She is aware because she also is like the rose. She is and the rose is. The rose remains in its nature because Meg does not do violence to the rose through the concepts of language. She allows it to lie before her and yet she takes it to heart as part of her own being.

She is also aware that the rose will die because Willy had plucked it from its stem. "It was to perish and no longer greet the sun, or dance and reflect the sunset." Willy had plucked the rose, and it would die; she would die, too, just like their relationship had died. She and Willy could no longer dance nor greet the sunsets together. She releases the rose, and thus everything in her world that has value to her, into its particularly. Thus, all attachments vanish.

Does the is-ness of Maggie's existence allow death to also exist entirely in what it is? Could this be the case only with Maggie's not naming the rose? Perhaps Maggie does not need to attach symbols of love, truth, and beauty onto the rose because she, herself, represents these abstractions. Perhaps she not only represents them, but also, they are part of what Maggie is. She no longer needs to execute or become the ideal. The ideal does not exist only in her mind, since she too is there in the gathering of all that is.

In the hope of making further sense of this language we move to Emily Dickinson's poem "Because I Could Not Stop for Death," the poem alluded to in "Leave Taking." The ambulance, now changed into the famous carriage of death, is waiting. Dickinson personifies death in this poem as a genteel Amherst gentleman caller, and Immortality is the chaperone. With this poem, Dickinson attempts to imagine an inside view of death.

145

In "Leave Taking" I also attempt an inside view of death, but in both instances only the ambiguity of death is realized. Dickinson is concerned with the loss of identity after death and interested in preserving selfhood. Maggie is also concerned with her personal identity as she passes by her familiar world, her world in time, that is so real to her. She passes this world on her ride with Death and then she passes the sun.

In this way she goes past time itself. But what is this time that she is passing? Has she not drawn all time to her, until time only exists in the gathering? If this is the case, then perhaps there is no time to pass, no sun to leave behind. Memories surface like water bubbles, causing tiny ripples to dance, play and dart; thus, she is there in time and she also flows in and out of time, "not dallying, moving, churning, not then, vanishing."

Maggie dies on the x-ray table. The "table had been cold, remote and unfriendly." All earthly comforts were gone. She no longer had the soft comfort of her pillow and bed, or the rose. "'Why have they done this?' she thinks. 'Can't they, don't they know what is happening?' She refuses to struggle for another breath of the life sustaining air -- she lets out the trapped air -- then refuses to fight for another.

In that split second between life and death she sees the stain on the nurse's meticulous uniform. She smiles as she sinks into death, because the stain is invisible to everyone, everyone except Maggie.

Then she is summoned down, down, and then up, up, and then it is all stain, all rose, all everything, and all nothing." Just what does this mean? There is yet another ambiguity: up, up and down, down. Upon losing consciousness she loses everything, including her ability to fashion ideas, exhibited in religious and traditional symbols, in the hope of bridging the gap between heaven and earth.

The stain imagery represents Maggie's essential nature of thinking, which is to transcend the immediacy of particular beings in order that this transcendence may reveal the particular in that which it is as a being. Without this duality, which occurs for a thing to be a thing, there is nothing. How close we always are to the abyss or to nothingness! This void speaks to us continually, not as something removed, but rather, as something close by and as a part of the essential nature of thinking.

Inauthenticity, on the other hand, seeks to avoid the abyss, by thinking in a way that encompasses the totality of all there is, a totality or wholeness that neglects the "is-ness" that continually arises and returns to that which it is.

The "is-ness" also speaks of everything -- everything and nothing. The everything is merely the conjunction between the stating and the saying or the letting-lie-before-us and the taking-to-heart of being. Without this conjunction, there would be nothing -- but instead there is everything.

"Then she is summoned down, down, and then up, up, and then it is all stain, all rose, all everything and all nothing." Nothing and everything, the ambiguity of death, the paradox. But death is, the rose is, and the stain is. All three are present in the world and, as such, all three are present to us, and so it follows that death is both everything and nothing, in the same sense that objects or beings, participating in our essential nature of thinking are both everything and nothing.

There is no need to understand this duality of nothing and everything. We only need to know it is there. There would be nothing without the duality, nothing without the return of particular being to that which it is.

Perhaps this glimpse into the "something" that is both everything and nothing realizes two possibilities for Maggie: either down, down into nothingness or up, up into everything. In this manner I do not deny, nor do I endorse, transcendence. I leave it as a possibility. In like manner, I allow the down, down into no-thingness as a possibility.

This inference reflects the nature of essential thinking that has been described above. Maggie also speaks of the nothingness in re-gard to her life as she approaches death. "'No, it doesn't mat-ter, nothing, nothing, and nothing. That's all there is,' she said as the hot demons struck her in the chest. 'Why should it please her so, such nonsense. Nothing? Why, how could this be? Surely there is something, always there is something, goings on and comings on -- people crying, people laughing, making love, eating, working, and on and on.'"

These lines represent Maggie's knowledge of the abyss, or the nothingness that is always there, and it seems like it is only the goings on and comings on taking place in the functional world that keep this reality hidden.

We can now perhaps understand another contrast between Willy and Maggie. Maggie recognizes the nothingness that is part of our existence, while Willy acts as though it does not exist because he conforms to the generality or totality of all that is.

Maggie also seems to escape many of the rules and regulations explicitly existing in the functional world. While Maggie did contribute to the patterns of the marital enclosure, ultimately only the patterns were left, a routine of sorts, a stalemate between them that took the place of a loving relationship.

She nevertheless lives uniquely. She is Maggie -- or rather Maggie is, the rose is, and the stain is. This quality is evident in how she reacts to the pain. She does not act in the traditional habitual manner, nor in the pattern of Christianity. She does not beat her chest in humble supplication. She merely accepts the pain and even swears, "'The pain, oh, the god-damn pain,' she muttered."

In this manner she resembles Ivan Denisovich from Solzhenitsyn's *One Day in the Life of Ivan Denisovich*. In this novel, Ivan is imagined as being completely unlike the Baptist Christian, Alyoshka, who actually rejoices at being in prison because it gives him the opportunity to think of his soul and offer his suffering to God.

Ivan in contrast lives in the prison world merely to survive and does not conjure up ideals of how to live, nor does he look toward heaven for future rewards. Ivan thinks about his boats, his cigarette butts, his wall, and all the little comforts that by our standards would be little or nothing, but he is thankful for them.

In a similar way, Maggie too is thankful for the comforts of her pillow, bed and garden. When these comforts are taken from her, as she is lying on the x-ray table, she sees the stain and because of this she is satisfied and pleased as she sinks into death.

Maggie's experience of her dying is presented as drastically different from the comforts offered by Christianity, where eager ministers endeavor to help poor souls into heaven. Their help closely resembles Willy's functional world, because all the goings on, including the religious symbols and rituals that are offered in recompense -- are offered in order to hide the nothingness that

148

surrounds everything.

Maggie realizes that they had missed this reality and wants no part of their endless words and rituals. She reacts simply to what is placed before her and then continues her journey past the sun.

Maggie is also part of the world. She relishes each moment. She remembers with sadness the loving caresses of Willy. She is closer to the earth than is Willy; she participates fully in the world and its "is-ness." Not once does she attempt to transcend this world.

Willy and Christianity are closely connected in their attempt to transcend death, or the nothingness. They are removed from Maggie's essentiality. But it is important to note again that her experience of essentiality does not transcend Willy's mode of being in the world; rather, we need to remind ourselves that they are two dimensions of meaning which co-exist in actual everyday existence, and as such they are necessarily interrelated.

Ironically, it now seems that Willy's prosaic nature attempts to transcend the world, while Maggie's essentiality transcends particular beings only so being can be that which it is, no more and no less.

Willy confronts nothingness following Maggie's death. There are therefore two deaths, the death of Maggie and the death of the patterns of their life together. Willy's life consisted of these patterns of external things. He clung to these "things" because they gave him the "life" that he lacked.

Willy was not consciously aware of this nothingness, this emptiness within him, until he realized that Maggie was dead and, with her death, the patterns, the "things," that cemented their relationship, also died. "His body felt heavy and he was cold. He pulled the colored afghan up around him and snuggled into the hollow left there by Meg's body. He clung to this space as though she were there to caress him. Shadows of tears touched upon his face, gripped into him, not letting go."

He curls up into the nothingness that he is; he becomes the particularity of his own unique existence. He is nothing, and Maggie now touches him completely and fully in her leave taking. He does not seek avenues of escape; thus, he closes the gap between life and being. Willy and Maggie are no longer in two different sites.

# References

Camus, A. (1962). *The Myth of Sisyphus*. (Trans. J. O'Brien.) NY: Vintage

Dickinson, E. (1960). *The Complete Poems of Emily Dickinson* (Ed. T. Johnson.) NY: Little, Brown, and Co.

Heidegger, M. (1962) [1929]. *Being and Time* (Trans. J. Macquarrie.) NY: Harper and Row.

Heidegger, M. (1968) [1954]. *What is Called Thinking?* (Trans. F. Wieck and J. Gray.) NY: Harper and Row.

Heidegger, M. (1971) [1960]. "The Thing" In *Poetry Language, Thought*. (Trans. A. Hofstadter.) NY: Harper and Row.

Heidegger, M. (1971) [1969]. "The Way to Language" in *On the Way to Language*. (Trans. P. Hertz.) NY: Harper and Row.

Solzhenitzyn, A. (1963). *One Day in the Life of Ivan Denisovich.* (Trans. M. Hayward and R. Hingley.) NY: Bantam.

# The Sense of Death in Life in
# "Up or Is It Down?"

In the story "Up or Is It Down"? Bennie struggles against the sense of death in life surrounding him. His only weapon against the ignorance of humankind in general is a dialectical questioning through which he attempts to make some sense of his world. In this manner Bennie has begun to question existence.  He is searching: "Who is Bennie? Where is he going?"

Bennie is seeking the "other" of his existence. Only Bennie can discover his own particular existence. His questioning does not necessarily reflect perception of the senses, e.g., simple perceptions reflecting sensations, imagination, passions or of the intellect.

The inner conflict is more like a mood resembling feelings of dread and nausea, reflecting Kierkegaard's concept of dread and Sartre's term *nausea.* Dread, defined by Kierkegaard, is a fear of nothingness or death, and does not relate to any particular object in the world.  Mood as a sense of nausea parallels Roquentin's nausea toward the world in Sartre's book *Nausea.* Mood in this mode reflects a general weariness or dreariness of everyday existence. Mood is the experience which discloses concrete being to Bennie overall, the complete fallenness of being in the world.

In this manner Bennie is like Everyman, since Everyman has been thrown into the world where a set of facts about himself defines his circumstances. Some of these facts include Bennie's environment teeming with people who seem incapable of understanding other possible modes of existence.

In this manner these "others" are caught in the web of the socialized man. This general attitude toward the world is seen in "Up or Is It Down?" as a sense of death in life and corresponds to Willy's attitude toward the world, the totality of all that is in "Leave Taking. "

Bennie's rash occurring at the sight of a dead body symbolizes his mood, or dread against the inner nothingness, or complete fallenness of being in the world. Luke's body, appearing to both Bennie and Irma as being the deadest body they had ever seen, discloses that Luke is in fact dead; in an inner sense even while alive and in physical death he was, therefore, the deadest person Bennie and Irma have ever seen.

Bennie's dialectic questioning relates to the fundamental characteristic of thought, which means, broadly, reasoning which exhibits the back and forth movement of debate.

As described more precisely in Kant and Hegel, it is a movement of negation and contradiction, from one point of view to its opposite and back again. In dialectical language individual statements can never be understood or taken to be true on their own, but only as moments in a movement of thinking.

Bennie's inner conflict has been described as a mood conveying feelings of dread and nausea. This nothingness and dreariness of Bennie's life encompasses a mode of in-authenticity where others create a stage or enclosure reflecting a sense of "death in life." The only means of self-identity is to create mirror images of each other, perpetuating the ignorance of humankind in general.

Perhaps a poem will help to illustrate this "sense of death in life," a sense that, unconsciously, adds momentum to Bennie's mood or attitude of being in the world.

> Will they measure, manipulate,
> Force a being into a space?
> A space so small it cannot grow?
> Horrible to contemplate
> When this being, they have made
> Moves about to do their bidding,
> Moves about at beck and call,
> Finds they turn away in hate.
> A reflection of themselves too late.

Bennie's intellect and sensory faculties offer him no consolation or help in this struggle against being forced into a space too horrible to contemplate. He does not want to sink beneath the tide, the stream, the sea, or whatever is the name of this thing that pushes him down and lets him drown. He is at a loss. He cannot rely upon his intellect or his sensations to understand or discover some object, something concrete to fight against. No, there is nothing, only a mood that keeps poking and tearing at him.

The itching symbolizes this "something." "The itch feels like something' real bad is trying' to git under my skin, tryin' to crawl right under thar and grab me an pull me down into somethin' I knows I won't like." The "somethin' real bad" is the forcing of a being into a space too horrible to contemplate. His being screams out, screams out as he stares at Luke's body, and breaks out in a rash. "It was a big 'un like a strawberry, an' as red as one":

Bennie's rash symbolizes his unconscious fear of the complete fallenness of being in the world or of a nothingness that reflects a person's refusal to understand or question existence. Willy experienced a feeling of nothingness as he fell into the hollow left by Meg's body.

As was mentioned, individual dialectical statements can never be understood, or taken to be true on their own, but only as moments in a movement of thinking. These moments, occurring within Bennie's stream of consciousness, represent Bennie's only weapon against the denseness that seems to draw him down into something he knows he won't like.

The up and down dichotomy is used in the story to reveal Bennie's inner dialectical stream of consciousness. The up and down contrast deals with the ambiguities of life, or good and evil, as Bennie searches for something stable, some absolute, or an authentic turning that would offer him a solid foundation, conducive to inner growth.

He is, instead, trapped in the general notion of socialized men. He attempts to make sense of such a contrary world by using his inner dialectal dialogue to question his existence. Is it up or down to die? Humans are both good and bad, or up and down. Luke is so dead that "God almighty, can't raise him up anywheres or that the devil can't pull him down anywheres."

The up and down imagery is also depicted in a subtle, humorous manner as Bennie confronts the concrete world of directions. The boy seems confused as to whether it was up or down the road to Luke's place. In the beginning he admits that he speaks and thinks in ambiguities. "I like being outdoors, even then, at times I want to be indoors."

The "others" in Bennie's life talk, think and act in an absolute or either/or manner. His mother calls Bennie lazy after she discovers him hiding under the table. She says he will turn out like

153

his Uncle Henry. She is, however, really not thinking, not thinking at all. She speaks from an in-depth programming that determines her behavior. She treats her son exactly as she has been treated.

Such behavior can perhaps be described as absolute in nature because it is devoid of the ambiguities that must be present to question one's existence. It is only in the moments in a movement of thinking that one can embrace unedited truths, adding depth and dimension to one's existence.

Just so, the storm that beats him against the wall of hopelessness also appears in the form of name calling, symbolized with the dog image. Ma reprimands Bennie in an indirect manner because she addresses him in a condescending and derogatory fashion when she discovers Bennie hiding under the table. She says, "Yer jest like some ol dog layin' 'round lazy. Yer lazy, that's what. Yer goin' to turn out jest like yer Uncle Henry."

Henry was hanged for thieving. As Bennie hears this unnatural tone, he changes her into a nanny goat and a crow, and he hates her. "Crissakes, the ole nanny, how I hate her when she's like that. She's not my ma then, no siree."

No, Bennie can't unravel whether it is up or down with grownups, or which side is up--the good side, or the bad side. His ma again refers to Bennie, in the end, as a dog. "She told me this, 'Now stay." like I was some ol mangy dog."

This disparaging circle is as deeply rooted as the marital patterns in "Leave Taking." Bennie's pa calls his ma lazy; Luke treats Irma like a dog, and ma uses the dog image while scolding Bennie. Irma orders Luke out on the porch to die and then feels guilty. "I wouldn't even order a dyin' dog out like that." And on and on, continually, each attempting to force the other into a space, similar to their own determined situation, too horrible to contemplate.

Bennie hates his mother's unnatural tone of voice because this voice reflects the mood, the nausea, penetrating the very core of their existence. It is as though the self is beaten against a wall. There is no place to hide, no escape from the formidable incorrigible *something*. She beats him down, exactly as she, too, has been beaten against the wall of hopelessness, down, down, into the nothingness, into a death-like existence.

But Bennie clutches there, grasping, scratching to gain a hold, a hold on himself, and he hates the ol' nanny goat. "It gits mighty, yes, godawful, almighty confusin' tryin' to sort out everythin' down here or is it up here in this world."

This mood is thus seen as a confrontation of facticity, while the dialectic movement reaches for something *other.* The facticity defines one's situation in life. Bennie didn't pick his parents. He was born of people at a particular time, in a particular historical epoch, in a particular society with whatever genetic structure he was given. With this he must fashion a life. The contingency of Bennie's life is deeply rooted in inescapable facts.

Yet, Bennie is capable of reaching for something other. This other represents a struggle for perfection that takes honesty and completeness as prerequisites for the possibility of wisdom, or for the possibility of useful dialogue. These insights, feelings, experiences, and actions satisfy our deepest concerns about the ends of life. They make us happy and conveys a comprehensive truth: Wisdom.

The death image in "Is It Up or Is It Down?" shows the extremity. Bennie's rash reaction to dead bodies represents the nothingness and dreariness, the facticity of his life, or the sense of death in life surrounding him.

Humans, in this mode, are like bees swarming around the hive, all working and acting but incapable due to the activity of their everyday world of seeing themselves as they really are. Their acts are blind acts. Humans, caught in the functional world, refuse to ask the question of being. Death in the story, therefore, does not represent physical death, but, rather, death of the spirit.

Irma Geiger, however, begins to wonder about her existence, because she, too, recognizes Luke's "deadness." Bennie notices this also and thinks, "But ol' Luke, here, he was the deadest person I ever seen. Can't tell why, but knowed when I seen his face, all a gray color." Irma states a similar recognition, "He sure enough is dead, never seen nobody look so dead."

Irma begins to recognize the nothingness of her existence-- "Her eyes stared out into the awful nuthin'ness an' her mouth was pulled tight, making her face look all screwed up like." She resembles the wolverine when facing physical death.

Irma, on the other hand, faces the sense of death in life. She doesn't fully understand but the thought appears and with it some future questioning. For the moment she feels guilty; she has treated Luke worse than she would have treated a dog. She, however, has felt the mood of this death-like quality that enwraps the living, and it opens her imagination to new questions: "what if Tillie 's right?"

In "Leave Taking," Maggie's essential nature of thinking represents an individual's ability to obtain an awareness of the other that transcends the facticity of everyday existence, or of the "totality of all that is" as depicted in Willy's attitude toward the world.

Maggie's attitude or awareness frees her from the endless cycle of the general concept of humans together. These others can no longer influence her negatively. They can no longer force her into a space too horrible to contemplate. She escapes this death-like existence, and yet she does not transcend the world with abstract notions of God or eternal life. She remains fully in the world with a particularity that reflects the ontological nature of our participation in the world.

Hand lived fully in the world with a particularity that encompassed ambiguity. He knew the smells of life and death, of nourishing men like D. James, as well as men who brought blood and death to the old bull. He remembered the smells of goats, and his mothering Molly.

When he charged the phantom bull, who embodied all these conflicting smells, sounds, and experiences, his guts were on fire. He was total passion and intention. He had no conflicting theories of death.

When he caught the strong comforting odor of goats, and an arrow plunging in his heart, "he fell forward and toppled full length into the earth's giant arms, embracing and cuddling him as though Molly is near, and the warm liquid is oozing out and a-round his soft muzzle." Both life and death have been fully engaged.

Bennie's human consciousness, of course, does not allow him Hand's simple awareness and passionate existence. Bennie struggles to gain a similar status to that of Maggie, but it is uncertain whether he escapes the facticity that threatens to pull him down into something he knows he won't like.

We know that he fights vehemently against this something. As his consciousness seeks self-consciousness, he compares external events, objects and others with his own inner dialectic movement. His thinking is uncanny, and resourceful. He is continually reaching and searching for answers, penetrating the core questions of existence.

He thinks about death and feels he can wait, "No sirree, I can wait fer that" and "Can't tell if it's up or down, to die, I mean."

Bennie likes babies because "They jest act like babies. Now with big 'uns its a story with a different color alt'gether. A body never can tell if it's up or down with grown-ups or which side is up--the good side or the bad side." He likes babies because they are just babies, but on the other hand, he realizes that they will grow into adults and become up and down, good and bad.

It is as though he is looking for something substantial or for some grounding or absolute in the external world. In Bennie's thinking the idea of a mind or God governing the world does not help, because Bennie does not seek belief systems or abstract ideals to help fashion his chaotic world.

Bennie's dialectic thinking, therefore, is devoid of manmade absolute ideas, or concepts about the world. Bennie is in the world confronting whatever it is that might bring to mind thoughts of an absolute, only to leave it behind as new contradictions appear. He thinks of babies as an absolute because they are just babies. He then dismisses this thought with the idea that they will grow into adults.

He turns to the trees and feels better. He likes the trees. They respect one another and "they are jest there, not up and down." The trees now take on the aura of an absolute, but not for long. He continues his dialectic and quickly confirms another fact: Trees are rooted to the ground, and, consequently, they are not free to do anything else.

Bennie's thinking now flows into thought of an absolute and freedom. It seems only humans are free, because they can be either up or down. He now changes his thoughts and quickly compares Luke to the trees. "They're sorta dead." Yes, they are sorta dead like Luke, because trees don't seem to move or change. Then he immediately switches his thoughts, "not dead like Luke is dead, 'cause trees were never alive like as Luke was alive." But then, "trees grow, bit by bit."

Bennie's dialectic stream of consciousness not only compares people and babies to trees, but also compares a dead body to trees. The conclusion is that a tree isn't like a body because it was never alive as a body was once alive. Also, a tree is alive because it grows. The body is nothing, nothing at all, and does not fit into a category with other objects and things in the world. It is neither up or down.

If this is the case, then it follows that a tree, since it is alive is up and down, because as Bennie finally reasons, "A tree is both up and down--up in the air and down in the ground."

Bennie's dialectical thinking is honest and complete. He does not need ideals or beliefs to compensate for his lack of perfection. Instead, he reflects the world in a dialectical sense or movement, the only world he knows. He does not desire to transcend this world; he only struggles to gain a proper foothold. He only wants to win victory over the "sense of death in life" that wants to pull him down into something he knows he won't like.

This something is the nothingness, or the "the sense of death in life" that measures and manipulates, forcing a being into a space so small it cannot grow, horrible to contemplate, an image of itself too late. Bennie's involvement cannot be appreciated in terms of the language of essences (of "what kind of thing") but requires the narrative structure of a story whose end remains to be told. ("Who's Bennie? Where is he going?")

Bennie is seeking the other of his existence and only Bennie can discover his own particular existence. Only Bennie can travel through the narrative structure.

Bennie's wisdom reaches beyond the intellect and the senses, because as he begins to itch at the sight of a dead body, he knows, somehow, that all isn't exactly right in his world. He doesn't want to become lost, like the walking dead in his life. His being screams out. "The itch feels like somethin' real bad is trying' to git under my skin, tryin' to crawl right under thar an' grab me an' pull me down into somethin' I knows I won't like."

# The "I-I"s Have It

In this essay I take up the odd term "I-I" of the mystical tradition. It stands for a state in which one's common life becomes merged with what many thinkers have used many names to designate as a Larger, Organic, or Ultimate Self. I argue strongly that for this to be an authentic growth in consciousness, it must always include the messiness, concreteness and passion of our common, everyday self or ego. These qualities are found in abundance in the short stories of this volume.

I have always believed the abstract categories of philosophy must find expression and grounding in narrative chronicles. For the reader, these accounts and yarns might be enough. For those who are drawn to truth-seeking intellectual explorations, I provide this treatise.

To begin Thomas Aquinas stated that "The slenderest knowledge that may be obtained by the highest things is more desirable than the most certain knowledge of lesser things."

David Chalmers, a cognitive philosopher, feels that consciousness is mysterious, although cognition is not. He describes this as the hard problem of consciousness as it cannot be reduced to the systems in the brain. We can think of this as consciousness of the lesser things. He also seeks certain knowledge of this problem.

I, on the other hand, desire to grapple with the slenderest knowledge that may be obtained by the highest things. In this essay I will attempt to speculate concerning my image of the evolution of consciousness. Without being absurdly misleading, this image is the realization that the "Ought" is founded on the "Is." The "Ought" does not refer to absolute moral laws. Instead the "Is" and the "Ought" represent the "I-I" of the mystical tradition.

"In his books Ken Wilber occasionally refers to himself as "I-I," which denotes his puny, individual, mortal self and the cosmic, eternal Self, the "'Seer that cannot itself be seen" (Horgan, 65). Wilber attributed the term "I-I" to the Hindu sage Ramana Maharshi.

In his book, *Rational Mysticism* John Horgan describes an interview with Ken Wilber. In this informal conversation Wilber stated that "mystical maturity does not necessarily lead to psychological maturity. In fact, powerful mystical experiences can retard psychological development by giving you delusions of grandeur. But the personality that you had before you got your satori is the personality you're stuck with. If you're a geeky little toad, then you're going to be a geeky little toad that thinks he is God" (Horgan, 41).

The above is an extreme defining. But it does aid in allowing us to see the differentiation between these two inner realities. The "Is" can be seen to represent the messiness of consciousness or the phenomenal self, while the "Ought" parallels the higher self or mystical maturity. Conceptually, it is possible to view these two polarities as inner (phenomenal self) and outer (mystical maturity) as both residing in the individual.

It is the ability to bring ourselves in front of these two opposing realities in order to awaken and support an authentic evolution of consciousness. In front of the Ultimate Source everything that we are comes into question and becomes as nothing. It is a feeling of the nothingness and/or the messiness of oneself in front of the higher reality.

Mary Midgley in her article: "Pluralism: The Many Maps Model," quotes David Chalmers:

Biological theory has a certain complexity and messiness about it, but theories in physics, insofar as they deal with fundamental principles, aspire to simplicity and elegance. The fundamental laws of nature are part of the basic furniture of the world, and physical theories are telling us the basic furniture is remarkably simple. If a theory of consciousness also involves fundamental principles, then we should expect the same" (Midgley, p. 11).

In this quote Chalmers is looking for certain knowledge of the lesser conscious. As he claims that it is possible for a multitude of particulars (messiness of life) to become firmly tied to a set of invariant basic laws.

Medley's responds with the thought that by "proposing that the structure of consciousness must be fundamentally simple in the same way as physics, Chalmers tries to abstract consciousness from the complexity and messiness of life." (Midgley,11).

In his journals Ralph Waldo Emerson acknowledges the messiness of consciousness with these words: "A score of words and deeds issue from me daily, of which I am not the master. They are begotten of weakness and born of shame. I cannot assume the elevation I ought for want of sufficient bottom in my nature." (Moore, 73).

I claim that this want of sufficient bottom or the messiness of consciousness is necessary in order for the Ultimate Source to be firmly rooted in the world. If this messiness is denied or overstated in some manner, then its only recourse is to tag along like a mere appendage.

This was evident with the arising of the geeky little toad. It tags along as to gain its proper foothold in the world and thus you have the evolution of consciousness, which occurs when real unity exists between the "Ought" and the "Is."

Chalmers does not feel that the "I-I" system is the real anchor for consciousness. Further he states that there is not any advantage in investigating or including spiritual or mystical experiences when seeking explanations for consciousness. His search is aimed at the lesser knowledge of "what it is like to be such a system."

I in my search for the slenderest knowledge of highest things; feel that there are spaces or gaps in his thinking where it would be possible to assert the possibility of transcendent experiences.

"There is not to say that natural laws concerning consciousness will be just like laws in other domains, or even that they will be physical laws. They can be quite different in kind." (Chalmers, xiii). Does the thought of there being quite a different kind of fundamental natural law, allow a space for spiritual experiences?

For Chalmers the lesser problems are what he calls the easy problems. And these are easy to solve. Science of mind, cognitive science and neuroscience can solve the psychological and phenomenal problems of human behavior. These can all be traced to the system called the brain or can be reduced to the centers, synapses, and neurons, in the brain.

161

It is, however, certain that causation of behavior is accompanied by subjective inner life. The hard problem is how can a physical system such as the brain be an experience? Or we can ask: "something it is like to be such a system?" Chalmers claims that we cannot reduce inner "something it is like to be a system" to physical laws. He, therefore, feels that in order for these two disparate realities to adapt to one another a new unseen fundamental law of nature will eventually be revealed.

As for now, he feels that we are in the dark about how consciousness fits into the natural order. But what about the "Ought?" Can the higher transcendent *Self* as it unites with the "Is" or the lower energies, serve as a connecting link to fasten the causal side of the brain with the unseen causal?

'The slenderest knowledge of the highest things' forces me to ask: "What we are" in contrast to "Who we are." Thought implies questioning. To learn we must question our world. There are problems involved in asking questions about "What we Are," because we are already a problem to ourselves. Paradoxically we are caught between the question and the problem. We ask questions when we know too little. We ask questions when we want to know the how or what of something.

Humans cannot merely ask and then examine the facts because we are in the midst of a situation; we are all immersed in our own perplexities or the messiness of consciousness. We cannot, like Chalmers, search only for the simple, stable law of nature that will satisfy the hard problem. I argue this law must also include the logical necessity inherent in "I-I" system.

We are immersed in perplexities because we come out of the world, like leaves from a tree. We cannot step out of the world, although we attempt to do so when we reach for objective satisfaction. We are a total part of the world; we are, therefore, situationists. Too often we attempt to explain our situation as the "What we Are" in the same sense that one would explain a leaf or a rock, or some other material thing. It is mistakenly taken to be an accurate portrayal of our actual situation. The resulting questions and problems are "What we are questions."

These questions might yield a deeper look at "What we are," such as how a biologist might look at a rock or a leaf, but nevertheless the problem does not include the "Who we Are." Yes, we

162

can agree with Chalmers and Midgley in that a rock seen by physicists is made up of certain composite minerals and is an actual situation in itself. The body and mind are made up also of composite minerals and can be held to scrutiny according to these individual parts that make up the living organism.

But the great situation of humankind cannot be so easily defined. The problems that are expressed in anguish, in mental suffering, arise out of the experience of conflict between existence and expectation: "Who are we" and what is our destiny? The increase of the atomization of our knowledge of human kind, as within the external physical sciences, propagates a ghastly falsehood that we are categorizable according to limited disciplinary directives.

We must discern the difference between the phenomenal self, the messiness of consciousness in Midgley's words and the higher Self as described and experienced by the Mystics.

Chalmers asks the question: "If consciousness arises from the physical, in virtue of what sort of physical properties does it arise? Some have suggested biochemical properties; some have suggested quantum properties; many have professed uncertainty" (Chalmers, 56).

A natural suggestion is that consciousness arises in virtue of the functional organization of the brain. What counts here is the brain's causal organization; an organization that might be realized in many different physical substrates.

Causal organization is like the map of a city that depicts the streets, buildings, but is incapable of showing the activities of the people. Midgley describes this as reducing the painful chaos of the real city to a few straight lines and simple angles. Still, many people think that physics can reduce the muddled living world to an idealized mathematical form.

Likewise, the story of our lives, our talents, our struggles, disappointments, choices, joys, and intellects cannot be reduce to theories and formulas. I have coined the term "personage" for these facts of being human. The personage is very powerful and is a force that holds as its automatism's are strengthened by perpetual repetitions. The personage relates to "What we are." The person or the authentic Self, the inner Self of the "I-I" cannot be analyzed and parallels "Who we are."

163

A fictitious story, again without appearing absurdly misleading, will help us catch a minute glimpse into the crucial relationship between the personage and the person.

Rose Petal decides to visit Larry Longears, a well-known psychiatrist. She wants to discover something substantial within that "rings true." She tells Dr Longears the facts of her life. She has decided to reveal herself more openly than she has ever done so before. She tells him things she has never dared to say to anyone else. She wants to be sincere, gut-level sincere. She does so in hopes that he will help her discover this person who has been lost in the shuffle of the many factors, images, feelings and contradictions of the personage. She wishes to be shorn of all the deceptive appearances under which we all so easily masquerade in everyday life.

On the other side of the coin the "Who we Are" or the person as the true Self, is always a problematic question yet it cannot be separated from the personage. A strange relationship exists between the personage and the person. They are always linked together and yet the "I-I" remains distinct. Is it possible to catch minute glimpses of the person through the personage? If so, does this add another dimension of evidence to the problem of merely reporting spiritual experiences? Is it an authentic sharing that transcends the reportorial approach?

Larry can gather the facts of Rose Petal's life. This is of course valuable, necessary information. However, if Dr Longears jumps to quick conclusions or, worse yet, evaluates Rose Petal according to his own theories and/or methods of psychology, then he does her a grave injustice. It is not the registering of these details that count, important though they may be. Larry could go on accumulating notes and observations, but this would not reveal the mystery of the person or the "Who we Are."

It is as though the patient is being viewed as a picture under glass. What a nuisance the glass is, how it perverts and interferes, how it catches the reflection of the other only as object. Most importantly this necessary, objective inquiry or the whatness of the personage, helps to establish a bond if it achieves genuine sympathy, affection and trust. It is only through the openness and sincerity of Rose Petal that this can occur.

It is here, within this enclosure of authentic trusted communication that the learning about the other changes silently into an understanding meliorating the mere learning of facts. A light suddenly bursts forth from this encounter as Rose Petal now recognizes that she has been understood in a new way. In this beautiful moment the personage and person have met. Personal contact has been made with the discovery of the "Who we Are" an authentic glimpse that is not to be analyzed or answered.

Dr Longears can then use the facts to sketch a picture of the patient's temperament, her character, her personality, but this is a portrait explaining only the mechanisms of the mind, or the reporting of the "What we Are."

Hypothetically, Chalmers' reaction to this story would perhaps dismiss the subjective possibility of the "Who we Are." He would agree that our knowledge of consciousness comes from first-person experience. He would agree that there are the biological facts, and human behavior and the brain mechanism by which these are accompanied. He would conclude by stating that there is nothing in this vast causal story that would lead one who has not experienced it directly, to believe that there should be any consciousness.

Dr Longears was able to go beyond and recognize the mystery of the deeper self. Chalmers would perhaps place this reality as just another aspect of the behavioral facts, dismiss it as an unnecessary variable, or not see it as it would not be in his line of focus.

Is Chalmers looking to satisfy the apprehension of people with one more explanatory theory? The deeper self is a different order altogether. It is a desire for sincerity or trust, which is the prerequisite for a personal contact where two individuals meet beyond earthly concoctions. The authentic encounter speaks of a new order, which is outside history and time, a truth in its own right. It goes beyond the rational and touches the very core of the other.

The evolution of consciousness, therefore, must include or investigate this genuine dialogue. It is not some fully formed model of what consciousness is or can become and yet it is a logically necessary system or enclosure where subjectivity and intersubjectivity are causally apparent. It is simply there in the unique response and attitude between individuals. Do we want Chalmers' search for certain knowledge of lesser things to disclose consciousness only as another intellectual understanding?

The main concern of the evolution of consciousness is that all experience be added as evidence, which implies that without experience there is no evidence. The woman was expressing the depth of her human nature, which reflects the thought that we come out of the earth like leaves from a tree. Likewise, the spiritual is natural like the golden wheat grains of mother earth. It is the nondual grounding for all life.

Yet one cannot safely go high unless one also visits the depths. If the messiness of consciousness that Chalmers overlooks remains dark and deep, then the alchemy of our lives that would transform our experiences from plain emotion into a deepening of the self does not occur.

Wilber's example of the geeky little toad depicts this situation. We are then divided into a hopeful transcendent self and a miserable actual self. Rose Petal's story revealed her human side; this was a deepening of the Spirit within. She spoke even with shame for this human condition, making it chthonic and earthy. She was sincere in her sharing; she wanted to be recognized as a full human being in spite of the insufficient bottom of being human. It was within her scream for real life that she was able to connect with the hubris of the spiritual ascent without thinking she was God.

I have reached into some very complex issues here. My image or claim is that the "Ought" is founded upon the "Is." It is founded on the "Is" because without this grounding in the natural world and the consequent natural laws, the stories of our lives are told with naivete and narcissism.

It is not the lower energies that are the problem; it is when we allow these lower level properties to absorb the transcendent reality. What story would the geeky little toad tell about his life in comparison to Rose Petal? Would the story of the "Is'ness" of his life be told with naivete and narcissism, would his ego energy then absorb the abounding, splendid beauty of the transcendent reality? It seems evident that Rose Petal's sincere search for self allowed her to participate more fully within the "Ought" and the "Is. Conversely, the "Ought" no longer was merely tagging along.

Chalmers in his search for a fundamental law of nature is partially on the right track. I claim, however, that this discovery will emerge only when we are able to see the full picture or the "I-I" connection.

Midgley is correct in claiming that the messiness of consciousness cannot be dismissed so easily. The encounter with the sharing that allows the Self to be at least momentarily recognized, can only occur with the openness of the Self's acceptance of one's animal nature. The transcendent also becomes the hubris of the geeky little toad when we attempt to hide this messiness of consciousness.

Grabbing with the slenderest knowledge of the higher, I assert that the "I-I" can also be seen as a system that necessarily produces authentic Goodness. Does the contrast between Rose Petal and the geeky little toad attest to this? The "Ought" gains a strong foothold in the world with the former and is a much weaker attachment with the latter. Thus the "I" produces a necessary connection while simultaneously occurring in nature or the world. and is mysterious. These three characteristics can also be seen in Chalmers' "What is it like to be such a system?"

The following is an attempt to clarify "the slenderest knowledge of higher things," evident in the above:

The "I-I" as a system produces authentic Goodness. (The "Ought" in precious, fruitful, relation to the "Is.")

(a)      And, if Chalmers' psychological, phenomenal system, as seen in causal connections between experience and the brain, produces the necessary hard problem of "what it is like to be such a system,"

(b)      Then, these two systems are part of nature, necessary, and yet remain mysterious. Therefore, it follows that what is needed is both Chalmers' scientific thinking and an inward-looking mystical approach.

(c)      The resulting natural laws will not be like laws in other domains. They can be quite different in kind. However, if in the search to solve the hard problem there is a denial of subjective systems, the result is the destroying of all sense of the messiness, the preciousness, and the unique irreplaceability of the "I-I" system.

# References

Chalmers, David (l996). *The Conscious Mind in search of a Fundamental Theory*. New York, Oxford, Oxford University Press.

Horgan, John (2003). *Rational Mysticism.* Boston, New York, Houghton Mifflin Company.

Midgley, Mary (2002). "Pluralism: The Many Maps Model" *Philosophy Now*, March-April issue. England, Anja Publications.

Moore, Thomas (2002). *The Soul's Religion*. New York, N Y, Harper Collins Publisher.

# Thinking and Language

Much of contemporary philosophy revolves around the analysis of language, which many authors consider constitutive of who we are as humans. So, everyone who teaches must grapple with language and life. Here is another essay in which I try to bridge theory, experience, and story.

What occurs when an individual tumultuously becomes aware of the void or emptiness that lies within? Does this awareness, especially if it is sudden, create a new foundation for or an altered language, and if so, how is it possible to recognize or evaluate this subtle, yet powerful change in thinking and communication?

In order to illuminate the above, two fictitious characters have been selected, the Police Lieutenant in Victor Hugo's *Les Miserables*, and the writer and father in Ingmar Bergman's movie, *Through the Glass Darkly*.

In *Through the Glass Darkly* the father of the young incurably mentally ill woman disclosed his attempted suicide after experiencing his tangled inner life. This awareness had been gradual, due to the firm and stubborn development of his public persona. This ego had been fashioned quite ordinarily, as his clever personality, intellect and writing talents enabled him to be accepted by societies' social consciousness, which approved whole-heartedly his mediocre novels, pleasant and at times appropriately un-pleasant mannerisms.

Why did it matter, with all this social approval, that he was in-capable of loving those close to him? He was presentable in the same way that a new used car is presentable, as they were both sustained appearances. Of course, his children and friends knew the truth, but they belonged to that secret society formed along the mysterious ridge of never revealing truths that unfold beneath or above societal verities.

The writer's strong will to power could no longer sustain him with "seeming" to be presentable. He had crossed the line and re-cognized that he was far from adequate. Suicide seemed the only answer. He drove his car intending to plunge over a cliff, but the car stopped, with the front wheels dangling over the precipice, and swaying gently, like a mother and baby rocking. The man stared at death.

Unsteadily, but very carefully, he crept out and trembled violently against the cliffs side for many hours. His soul cried against the stones. Tiny mental fits struck the hard surface. And, like a deep call in the dark, he felt a tiny light, a spark: Was this some-how God? alive in the dark recesses of his being.

The black void was lessened as the tiny fits clung tightly to the light. Yes, he could slightly, ever so minutely, feel something out-side his public ego emerging. Afterwards, he began to feel genuine love and care for his family. But it was a small matter, certainly not the ringing of bells, or the hurrahs of a splendid religious experience. No, it was instead a quiet resolution to continue with life, to plod on somehow. Suicide was now unacceptable. The choice was life, or movement, ever so slowly "Through the Glass Darkly."

As he revealed this experience to his son-in-law, the husband of his incurably mentally ill daughter, a question implicitly materialized: How would he change his language, his writing to adjust to the new awakenings? How could he now proceed after many years of thinking and writing without the source that elicits true imagination? These questions were left unanswered. Time was needed to reconcile language and thought to express his new life. Habitual patterns of thought were too deeply ingrained, causing him it seemed almost unconsciously to repeat this inveteracy as he still sought to fill himself with the terror, pain, and at times, joy of others.

He was further appalled to discover that he wanted to record his own daughter's slow process into complete insanity. A muddled admixture of a new forming love and his old life line made progress tedious and awkward. But, how else to move except through the glass darkly? Everything, his very life, had been created with external stimuli. His language, complete with ideas, and beliefs were "tools" to express "what is", and in this situation the "what is" was the writer's total dependence upon something "other," the public world experience, and all other gathered commonalty that "seeming" rings true. The hidden unheard and unfelt world gives way to the perceived noise of the world; clamorous, feeding his poor brain, input, input, and the output into language and thinking forms.

> I see an old man get into a new Grand AM.
> I wonder why this is so.
> He jams it in gear and roars away, away
> Roars.
> And I wonder why this is so.
> Is it because the hidden, unheard and unfelt world sinks
>     low?
> While the heard noise of the world
> Roars away - away
> I wonder where is this away?
> Roar.

Perhaps the scientific materialists are correct, and the brain is like a computer, programmed with external data, and consciousness or the mind is the output. Of course, nobody yet knows how to derive minds and consciousness from matter. Thus, the principle of epiphenomenalism was added. According to this principle, all mental phenomena can be explained as epiphenomena, or secondary phenomena of matter by a suitable reduction to antecedent physical conditions. The basic idea is that what we call consciousness is simply a property (or group of properties) of the brain when the brain is viewed at a certain level.

When the writer drove his car over the cliff, he could be described as an epiphenomena phenomenon, as his consciousness was a mere programmed effect of his computerized brain. Cause and effect were in complete agreement. The material world was in control. There existed no dualism, just as the scientific material realists claim.

However, the macrocosm world of gravity did not fulfill its mean task, and what seemed like necessary death did not occur. Both the macro and micro principles of causation were jarred at its core, the car stalled, and the man's consciousness was severed from his computerized brain. The only apparent effect was the writer's huddled figure trembling against the rocky cliff, alive and yet dead as his consciousness was, so to speak, on its own.

Perhaps this is one of the problems with our modern world. We have no real connection with eternity, the unheard and unfelt world, and the resulting values that unify us to this transcendence present in the mundane. And if, for example in religion, the anchor of this transcendence is present only in the mind as idea, then we are moored to an illusion, and so we be-come lost in the infinite void, the "Roar away" that leads now-here. Thus, power is the only value that can take the place of this loss of value.

In the above the writer sought power to be something he was not. This is what Nietzsche and Heidegger meant by the "Death of God" the night of the world, or a temple without a shrine.

To touch reality is to gain a glimpse of eternity and this is to understand the gap or distance between ourselves and God. It is only then that we begin to think, only then does thought allow us to think. The man was now capable of looking out into the abyss, into the mystery, intuiting what was not himself. Yes, the void was lessened, but the human situation is muddled and complex. He would have to learn to trust this inner source, to be convinced that it would carry him forth into expanding regions of awareness.

The Police Lieutenant in *Les Miserables* committed suicide after discovering the absolute nothingness of his life. His life force evolved within his conception of good and evil. These concepts had been taught, especially through the example of his father who took him as a young boy to the prison where he work-ed as a guard. He, like the writer, grew up into egocentricity, computized by the external public game that demands that one must know.

He thought he knew all about good and evil out there. He had not summoned good and evil into existence for himself. He did not know that the choice was not the rival values of good and bad. His "will to power" was, therefore, this illusory conviction that he knew good and evil. But like the writer, he was actually con-trolled by the greater power of cause and effect. With a "roar" and "away" he perniciously arrested and condemned, without mercy, the down-trodden.

He was then shown compassion by the protagonist, a man he had been unjustly pursuing for years. This man had volun-teered to execute him as a foe during a revolutionary coup but

172

had released him. It took quite a while before the Lieutenant understood. He asked why he had been released. The person's reply was simply, "I pitied you."

The Lieutenant was then flooded with the terrible realization that his life was worthless. Silently he turned and walked towards the river. The poor, downtrodden social misfits, resting there, fled, as they knew him as a man without pity or compassion. Forgiveness and confession were not present in his language. He could only feel a great black despair, like a fog of the dark night settling over and around him. Without further ado he handcuffed his wrists and jumped into the river.

Heidegger felt that ordinary language was inadequate in expressing Being. For him, Being represented the field of openness surrounding us and revealing itself to us. We step out towards the future within this un-concealment of Being. If we do not recognize this movement, we then attach our thinking or language to the world in order to possess and control. He felt that a more dignified language or a poetic language was needed to express this reality of un-concealment, or ideally a Poetic Philosophy.

He disliked the vulgar talk of ordinary language. Poetic language would thus help create a sphere where inner can co-exist or fuse with outer and not be consumed into the brute force of material energy that places subject and object at war as one-upmanship divisions are constructed. This was his answer to the problem of metaphysics, as the "other."

The beyond is not some transcendent reality, but is rather Being, present in the world, existing as a non-concept that makes everything possible. This step-back allows Being as difference to come before thinking without being its object.

To express this as poetic language, a new language must be fashioned. Wittgenstein, on the other hand, disagreed. He felt that metaphysical language is meaningless. We cannot express what goes beyond language. We can only be silent and perhaps show, not speak of the transcendence.

We now have a contrary or different case, as the Lieutenant's silence was not the silence Wittgenstein spoke of. Nor was it a lack of poetic language needed to express Heidegger's unconcealment, or the revealing of his new awareness. Simply, it was an altered, yet ordinary language that was needed. To speak purely and simply to these oppressed people, "have a nice day" or "it's a fine day," was perhaps what was needed.

No! The simple, especially if it appears stupid, is most difficult. His ego was still there, clinging to the world. He did not have the special humility necessary to speak these brief amenities. Another difficulty was that this simple matter of speaking would have had to be repeated over and over in diverse modes and with the same humility. He could not do this, he was used to the speech of power and position. The only answer was his sensational leap into the water. If he had waited, like the writer, then, perhaps, some inner power would have helped him.

Therefore, it seems each touchstone of truth must be reconciled within language, but the wider the gap between the touchstone and our former language participation, the greater the despair. The Lieutenant's and the writer's language had been caught in the Great Materialistic Machine of the External World. In this sense, there is agreement with the material monists and their principle of epiphenomenalism.

Language is however, residual. When an inner change occurs a natural force or movement also occurs, which attempts to fuse the inner with the outer. This outer is not the brute force of the material world but is instead the unheard and unfelt world of beauty and harmony.

The problem is that of the residue language. From childhood on into adulthood language was slowly formed, until it reached an apex of consummation uniting the total person; body, brain, mind and consciousness. If a change occurs in consciousness, especially abruptly, as with the Lieutenant, language remains intact as the residue of the previous state.

This is why the lieutenant could not speak. The residue language was still there, beating against his skull like a sledge hammer. A new apex consummation with brain, body, mind and consciousness resulting in an altered language had not had time to materialize. It would probably take many seasons, with numerous people capable of this awkward, difficult, change before it could be recognized and utilized.

This pure and simple accomplishment would disallow the long-drawn out, sing-song monologues of Holy talk projected by the supposedly enlightened, or the long, equally dry monologues of most all discourse. It is not the true and false movement of propositions that discloses meaning reflecting inner truth. This participation can be expressed. It is only that we haven't the courage to proceed, to risk challenging the common-sense consensus.

Many are called, but few can actually cross the line that requires so much with so little beyond our inner, difficult to express knowing. Therefore, a limiting language dominates, and the Linguistic Philosophers are approved as they join with the material realists.

Author Note:

# Patricia Herron

**Patrician Herron** was born and raised on a ranch near Elgin, Oregon. She is a retired philosophy and religious studies professor who has taught courses in Oregon at Oregon State University, Marylhurst University, and Chemeketa Community College. She is the co-editor of *Spheres of Awareness: A Wilberian Integral Approach to Literature, Philosophy, Psychology, and Art*, and contributes to such journals as *Vision in Action*, *Philosophy Now,* and *The Humanistic Psychologist*. She is also a poet, artist, seminar lecturer, and lifelong seeker of Truth that can only be heard within the silence of the soul. This quest is apparent in her works of art and her teaching. "Life at all costs" is her scream. Communication concerning this volume may be addressed to the author at patriciaherron@juno.com or the editor at gregoryjjohanson@ gmail.com.

Made in the USA
Columbia, SC
01 June 2019